D0975788

by Tedd Arnold
Martha Hamilton
and Mitch Weiss

illustrated by Tedd Arnold

HOLIDAY HOUSE · NEW YORK

For Jeremiah, Mady, Zachary, Liam, and Ares
—T.A.

With gratitude to Linda & Walt,
who did the impossible
—M.H.

For Alan, my impossibly great brother
—M.W.

Text copyright © 2021 by Tedd Arnold, Martha Hamilton, and Mitch Weiss
Illustrations copyright © 2021 by Tedd Arnold
All Rights Reserved
HOLIDAY HOUSE is registered in the U.S. Patent and Trademark Office.
Printed and bound in May 2021 at Toppan Leefung, DongGuan City, China.
The artwork was rendered digitally using Photoshop software.
www.holidayhouse.com
First Edition
1 3 5 7 9 10 8 6 4 2

Library of Congress Cataloging-in-Publication Data

Names: Arnold, Tedd, author, illustrator. | Hamilton, Martha, author. |
Weiss, Mitch, 1951- author.
Title: Noodleheads do the impossible / by Tedd Arnold, Martha Hamilton and
Mitch Weiss ; illustrated by Tedd Arnold.
Description: First edition. | New York : Holiday House, [2021] | Series:
Noodleheads ; 6 | Audience: Ages 6-9. | Audience: Grades 2-3. | Summary:
After hearing Uncle Ziti's unbelievable story about a snake and a frog,
brothers Mac and Mac are captivated by the idea of doing something
impossible so that perhaps one day people will tell tales about their
amazing feats.
Identifiers: LCCN 2021001352 | ISBN 9780823440030 (hardcover)
ISBN 9780823450268 (epub)
Subjects: LCSH: Graphic novels. | CYAC: Graphic novels. | Fools and
jesters—Fiction. | Brothers—Fiction. | Humorous stories.
Classification: LCC PZ7.7.A757 Nok 2021 | DDC 741.5/973—dc23
LC record available at https://lccn.loc.gov/2021001352
ISBN: 978-0-8234-4003-0 (hardcover)

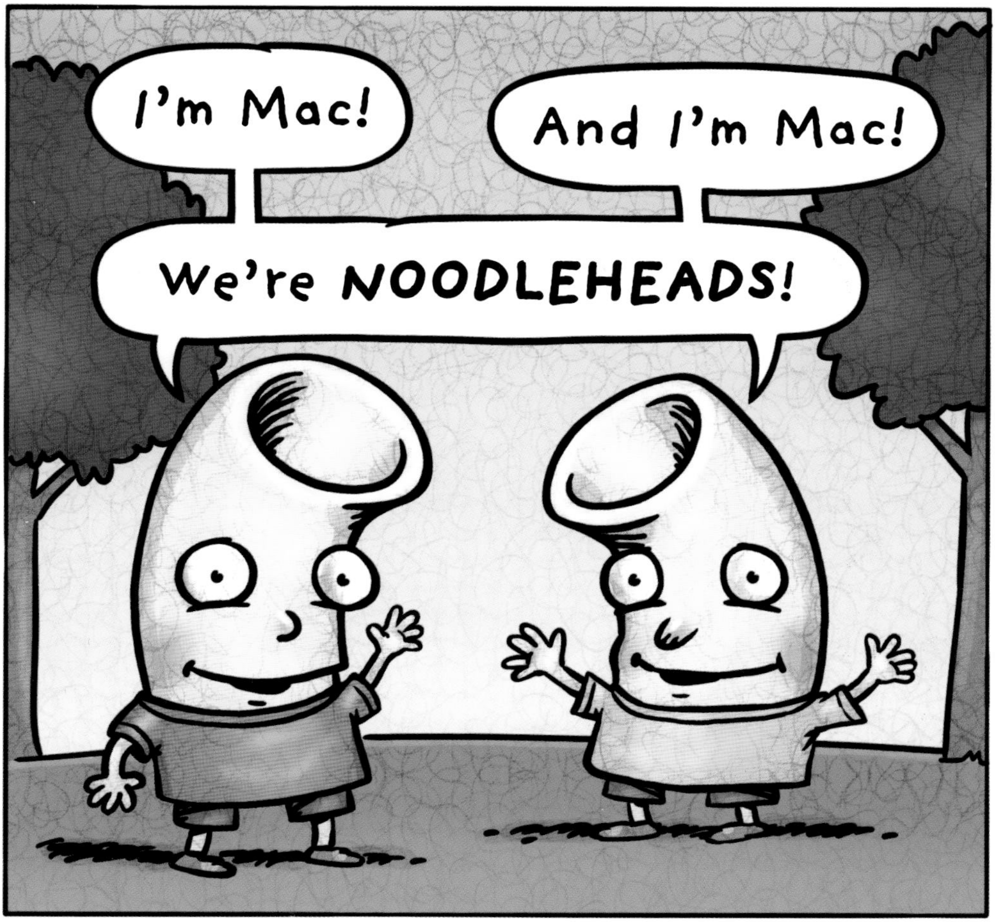
I'm Mac!
And I'm Mac!
We're **NOODLEHEADS!**

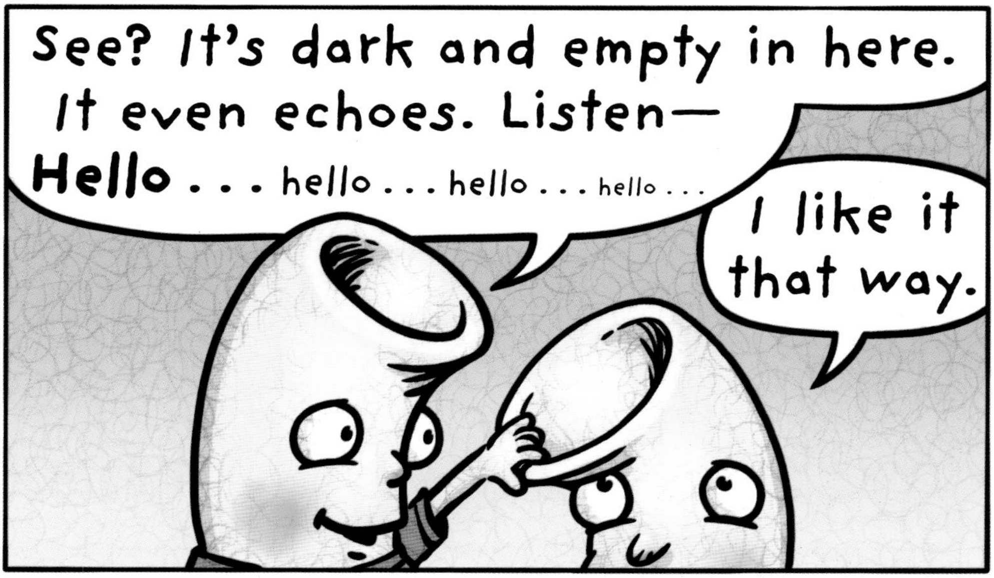
See? It's dark and empty in here. It even echoes. Listen— **Hello** . . . hello . . . hello . . . hello . . .
I like it that way.

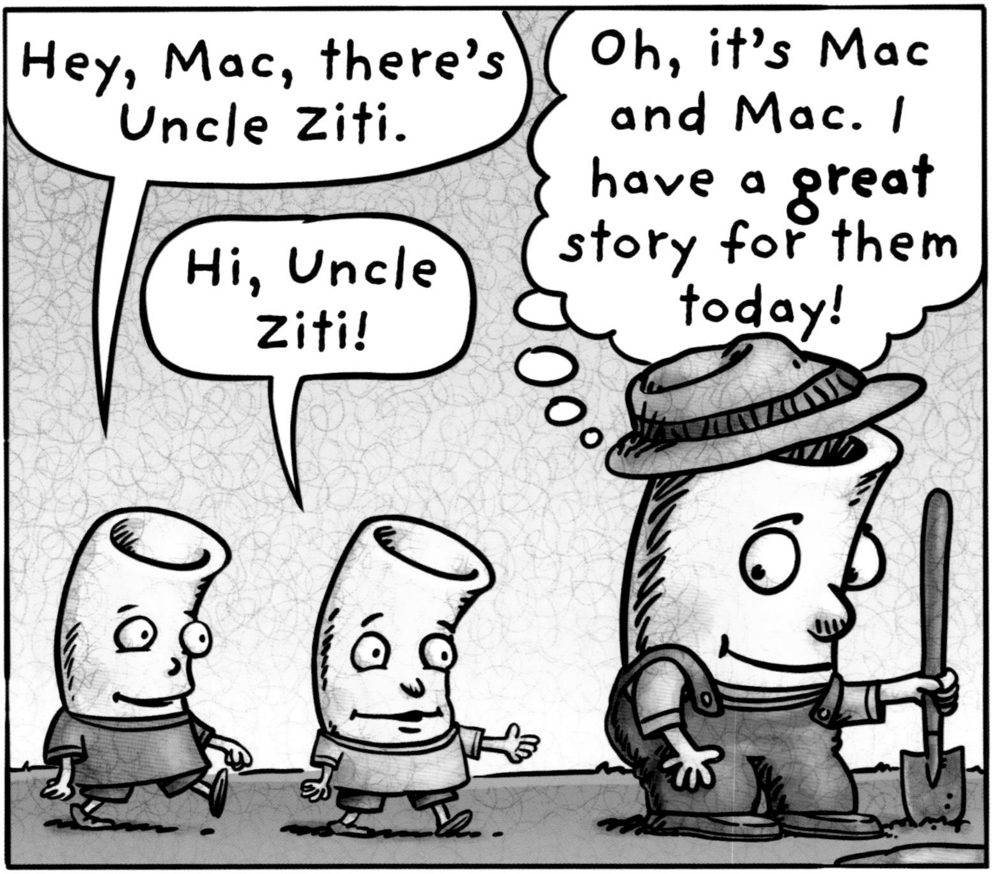
Hey, Mac, there's Uncle Ziti.
Hi, Uncle Ziti!
Oh, it's Mac and Mac. I have a **great** story for them today!

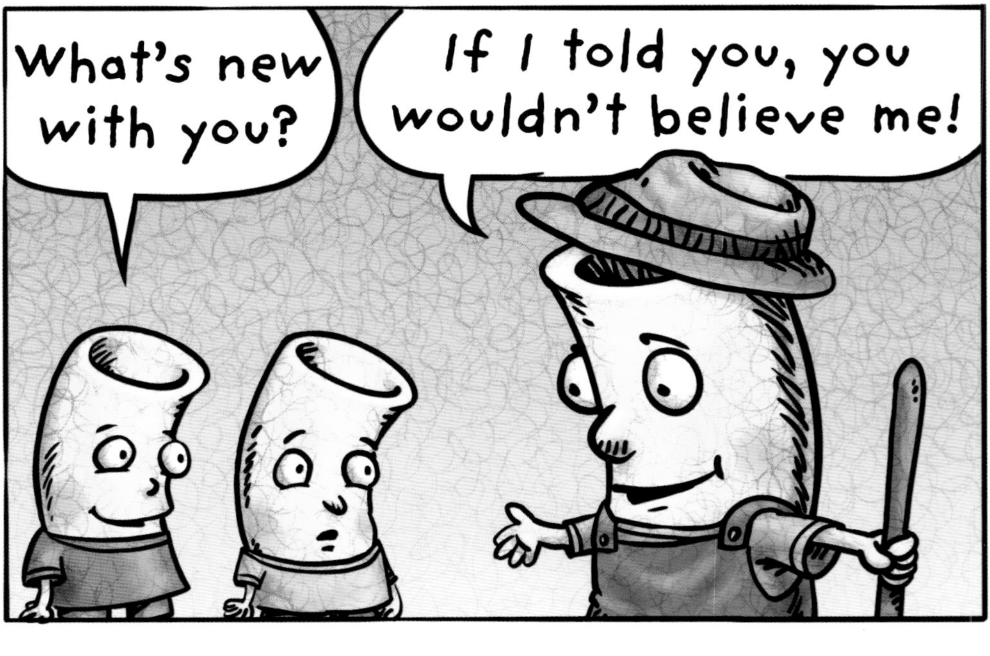
What's new with you?
If I told you, you wouldn't believe me!

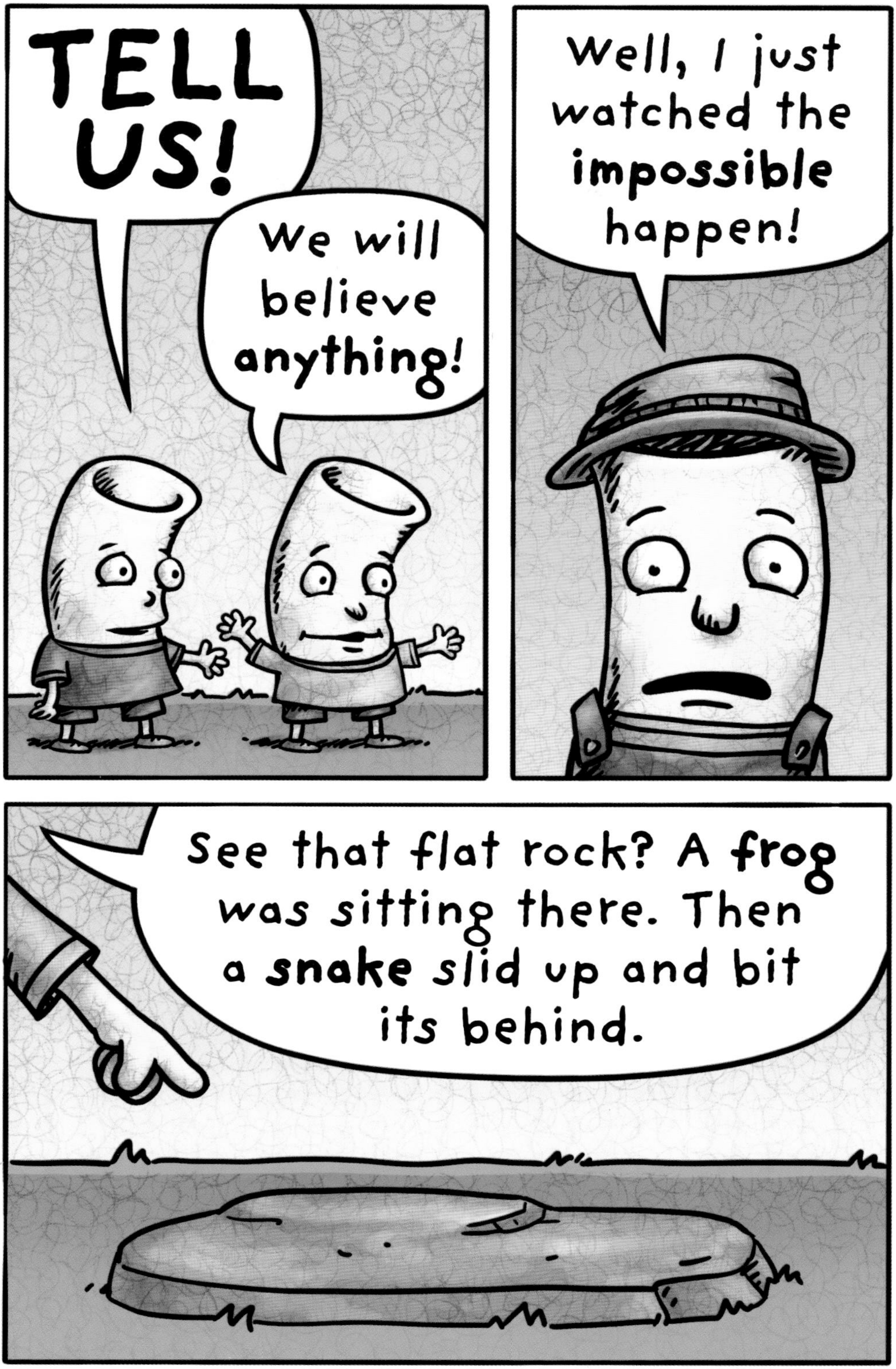
TELL US!
We will believe anything!
Well, I just watched the impossible happen!
See that flat rock? A frog was sitting there. Then a snake slid up and bit its behind.

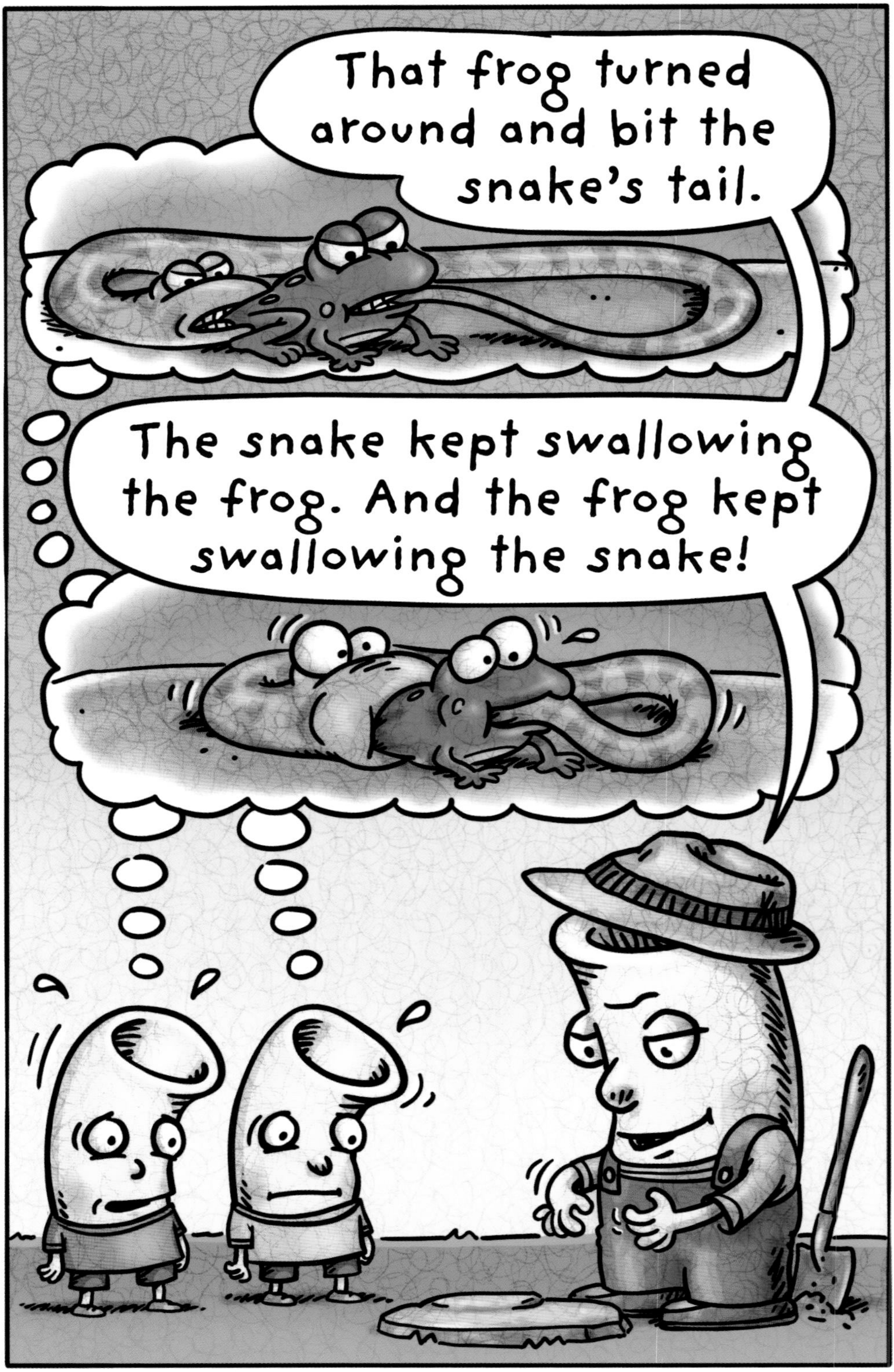
That frog turned around and bit the snake's tail.
The snake kept swallowing the frog. And the frog kept swallowing the snake!

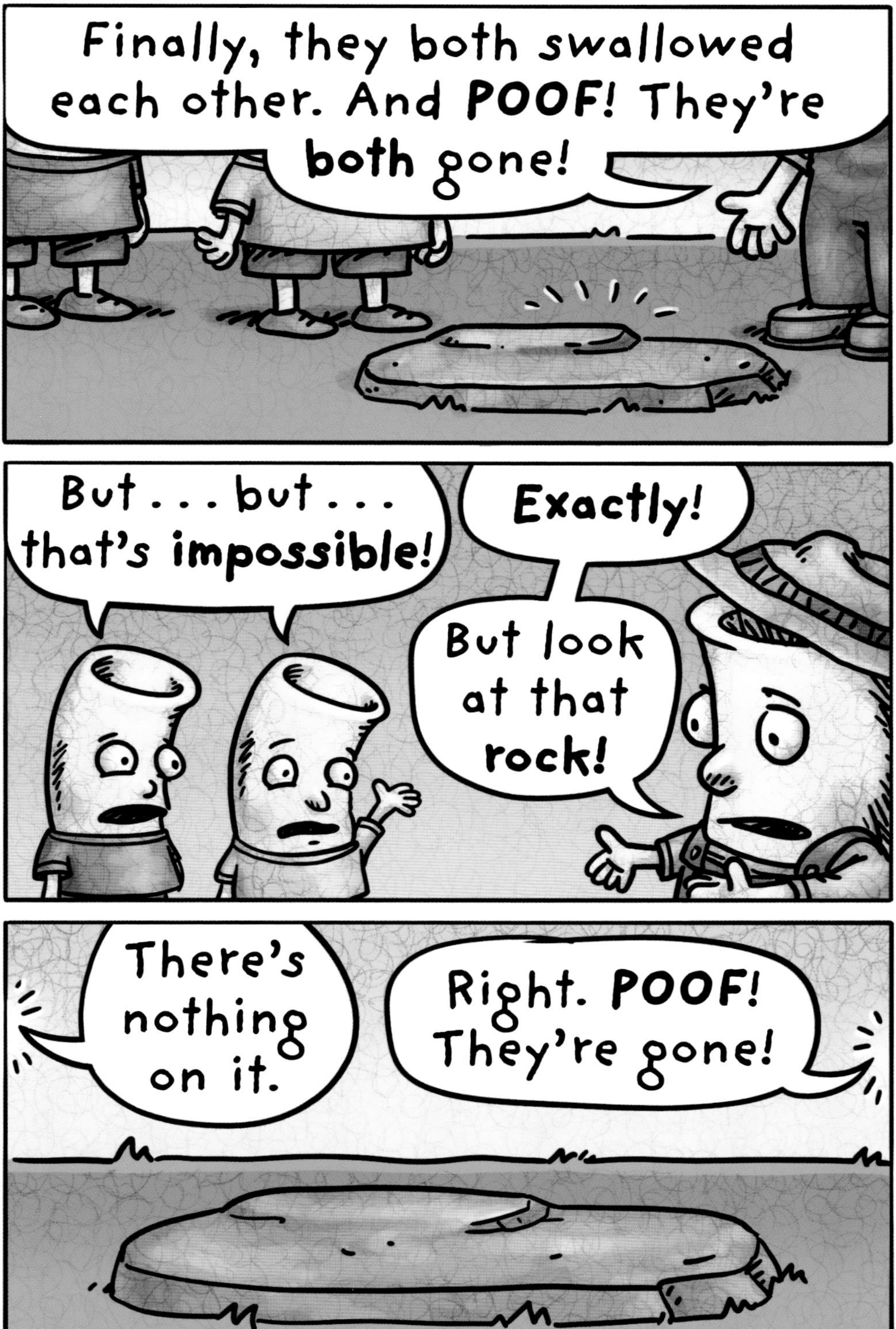
Finally, they both swallowed each other. And POOF! They're both gone!
But . . . but . . . that's impossible!
Exactly!
But look at that rock!
There's nothing on it.
Right. POOF! They're gone!

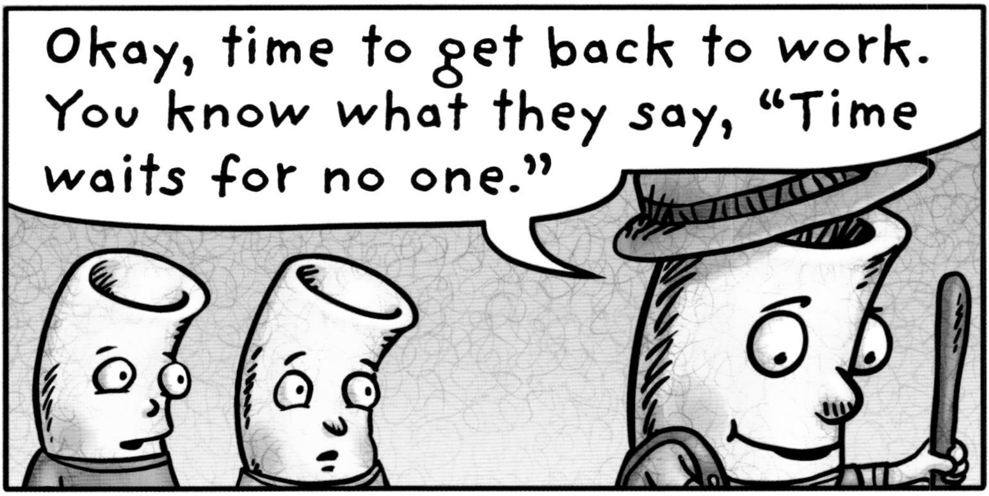
Okay, time to get back to work. You know what they say, "Time waits for no one."

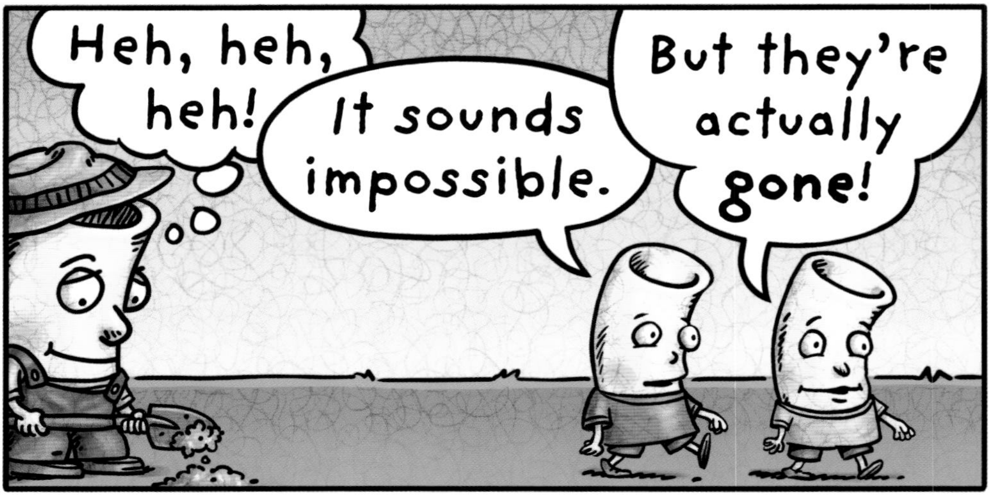
Heh, heh, heh!
It sounds impossible.
But they're actually gone!

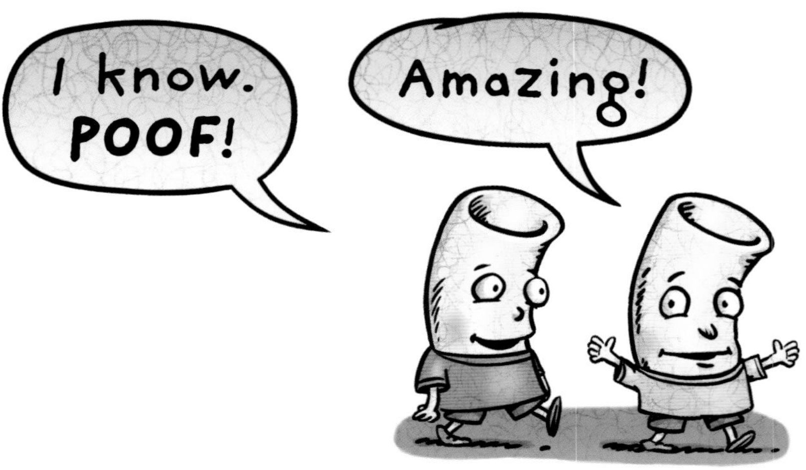
I know. POOF!
Amazing!

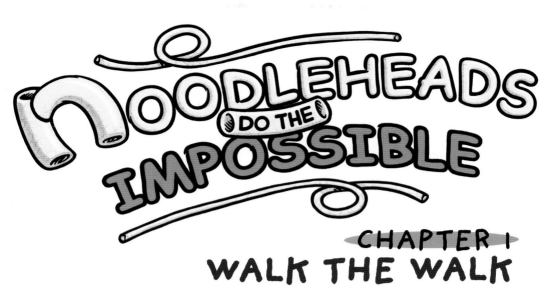

NOODLEHEADS DO THE IMPOSSIBLE

CHAPTER 1
WALK THE WALK

Uncle Ziti always tells the **best** stories!
Hey! If we do something impossible, people will tell stories about us. We'll be **famous**!

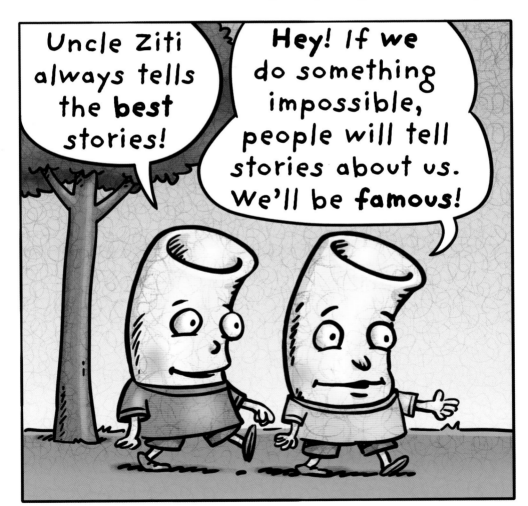

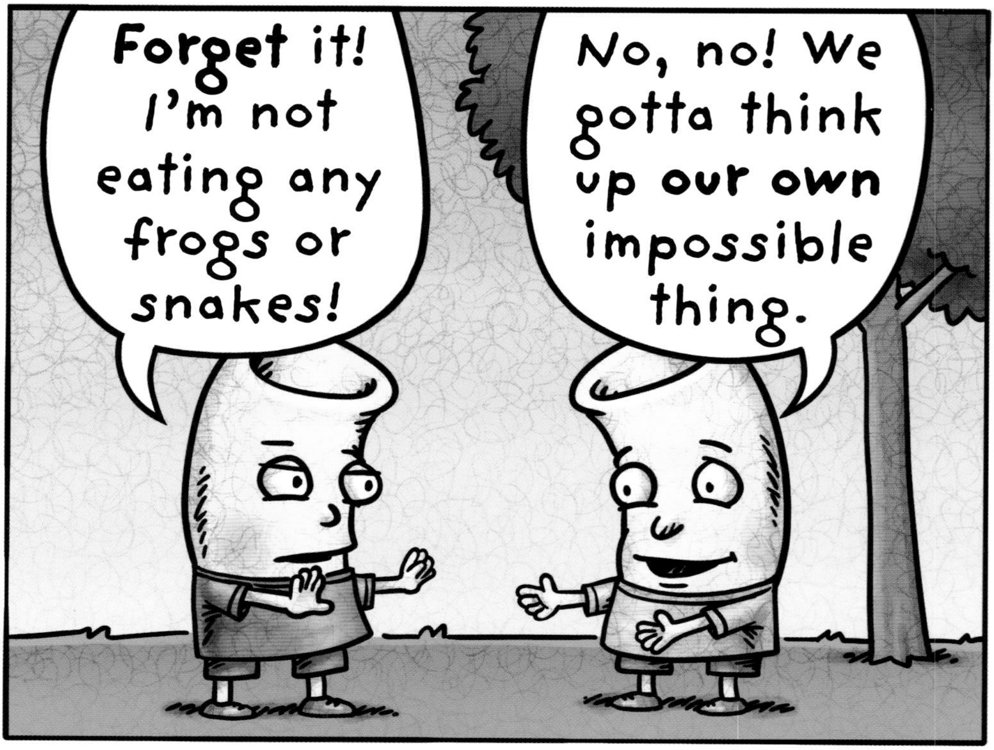
Forget it! I'm not eating any frogs or snakes!
No, no! We gotta think up our own impossible thing.

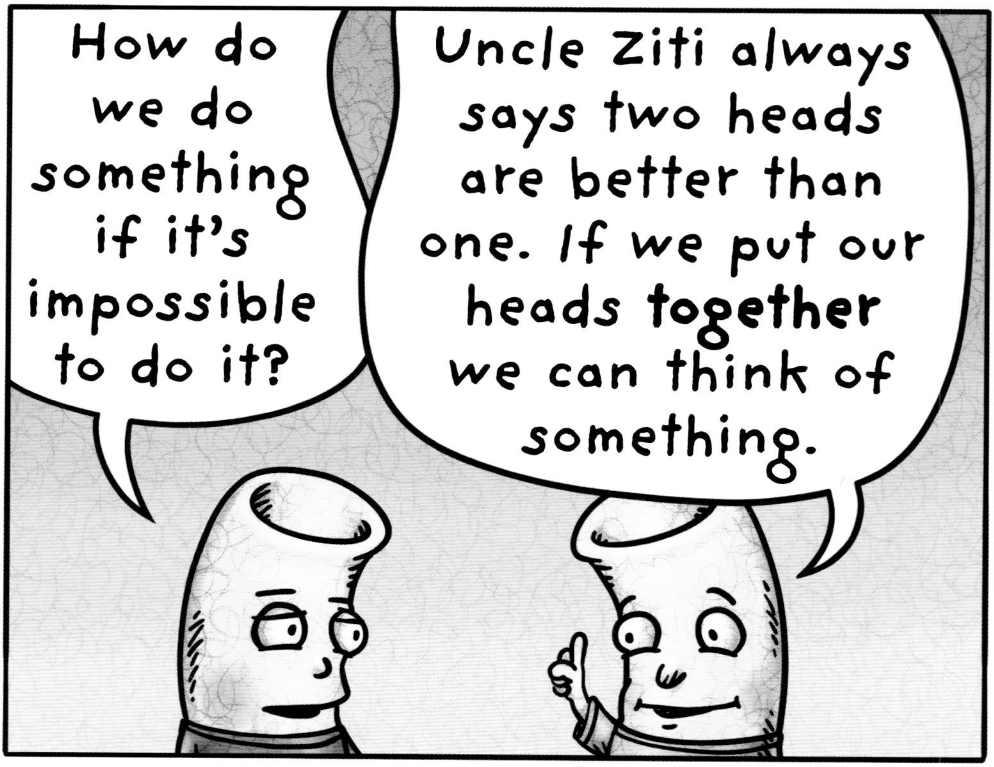
How do we do something if it's impossible to do it?
Uncle Ziti always says two heads are better than one. If we put our heads together we can think of something.

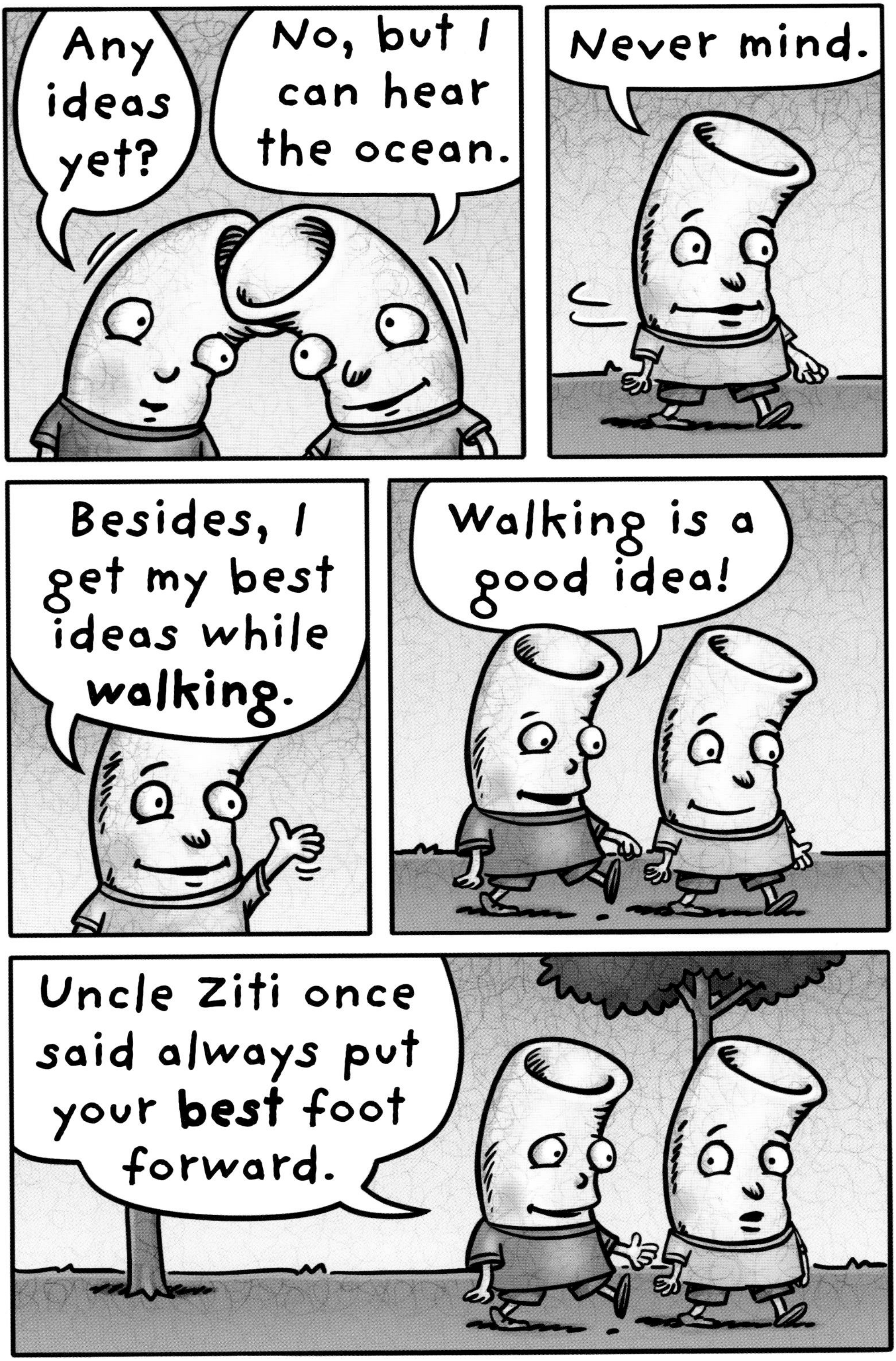
Any ideas yet?
No, but I can hear the ocean.
Never mind.
Besides, I get my best ideas while **walking**.
Walking is a good idea!
Uncle Ziti once said always put your **best** foot forward.

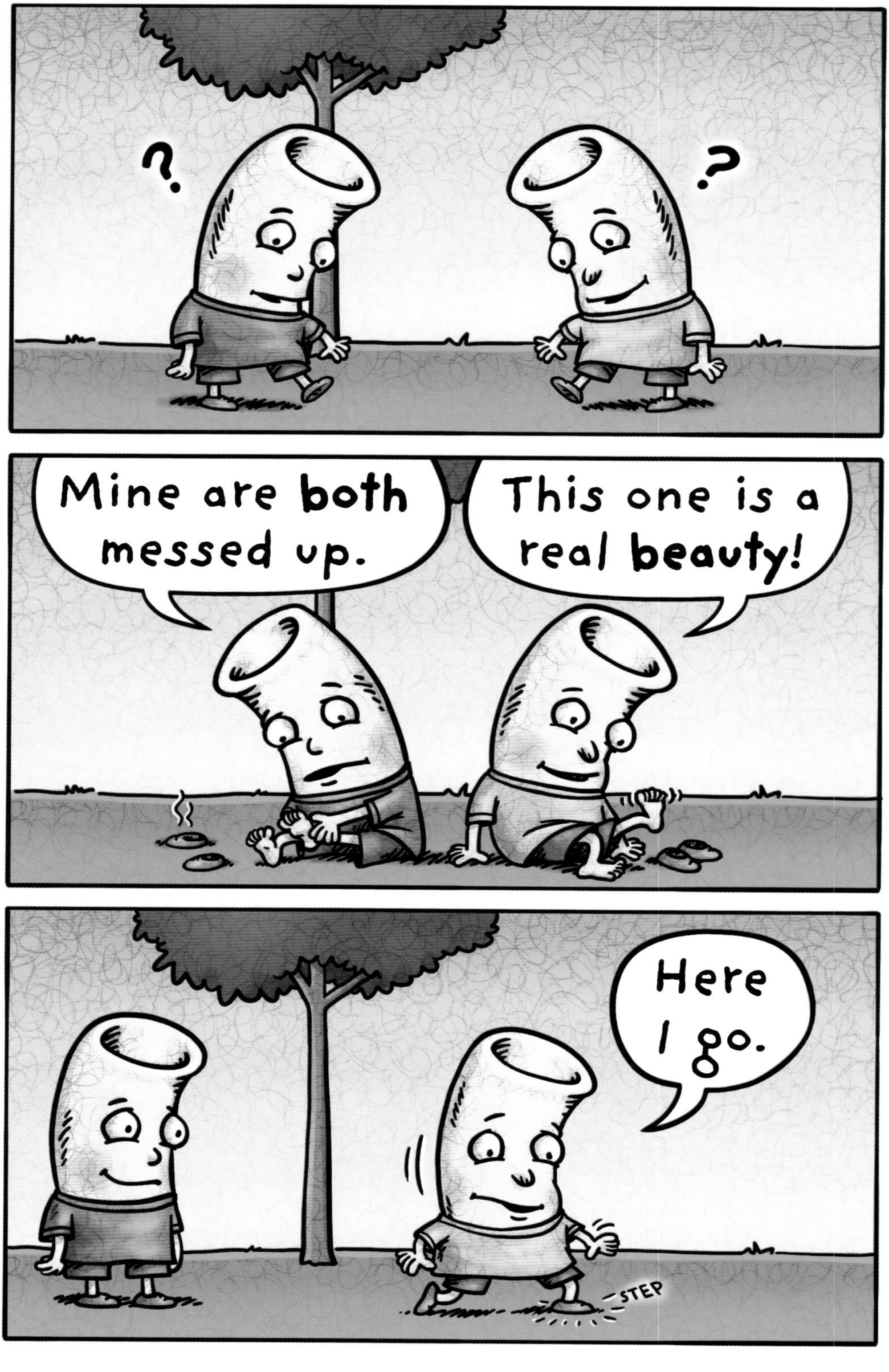
?
?
Mine are **both** messed up.
This one is a real **beauty**!
Here I go.
STEP

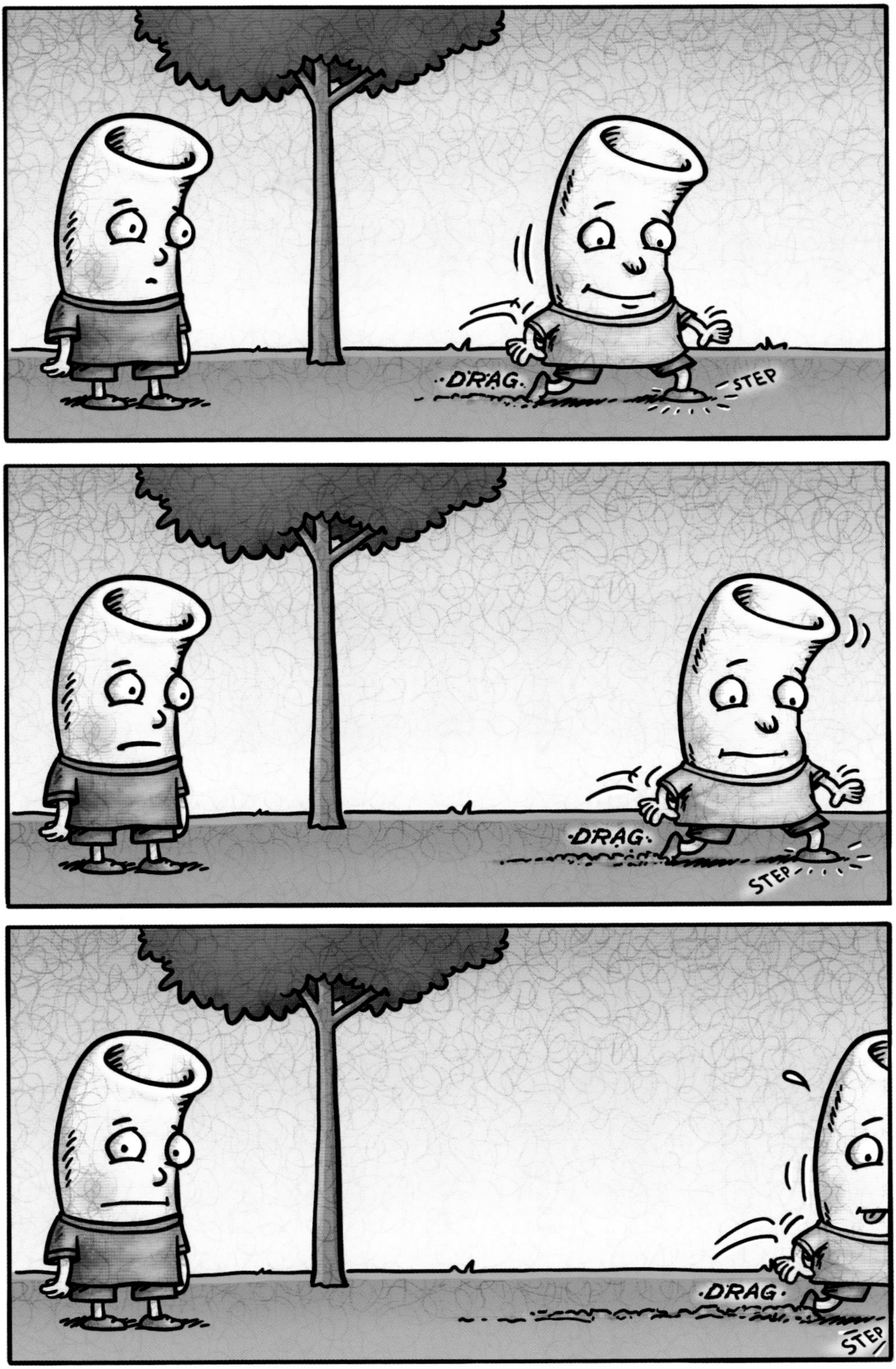
DRAG
STEP
DRAG
STEP
DRAG
STEP

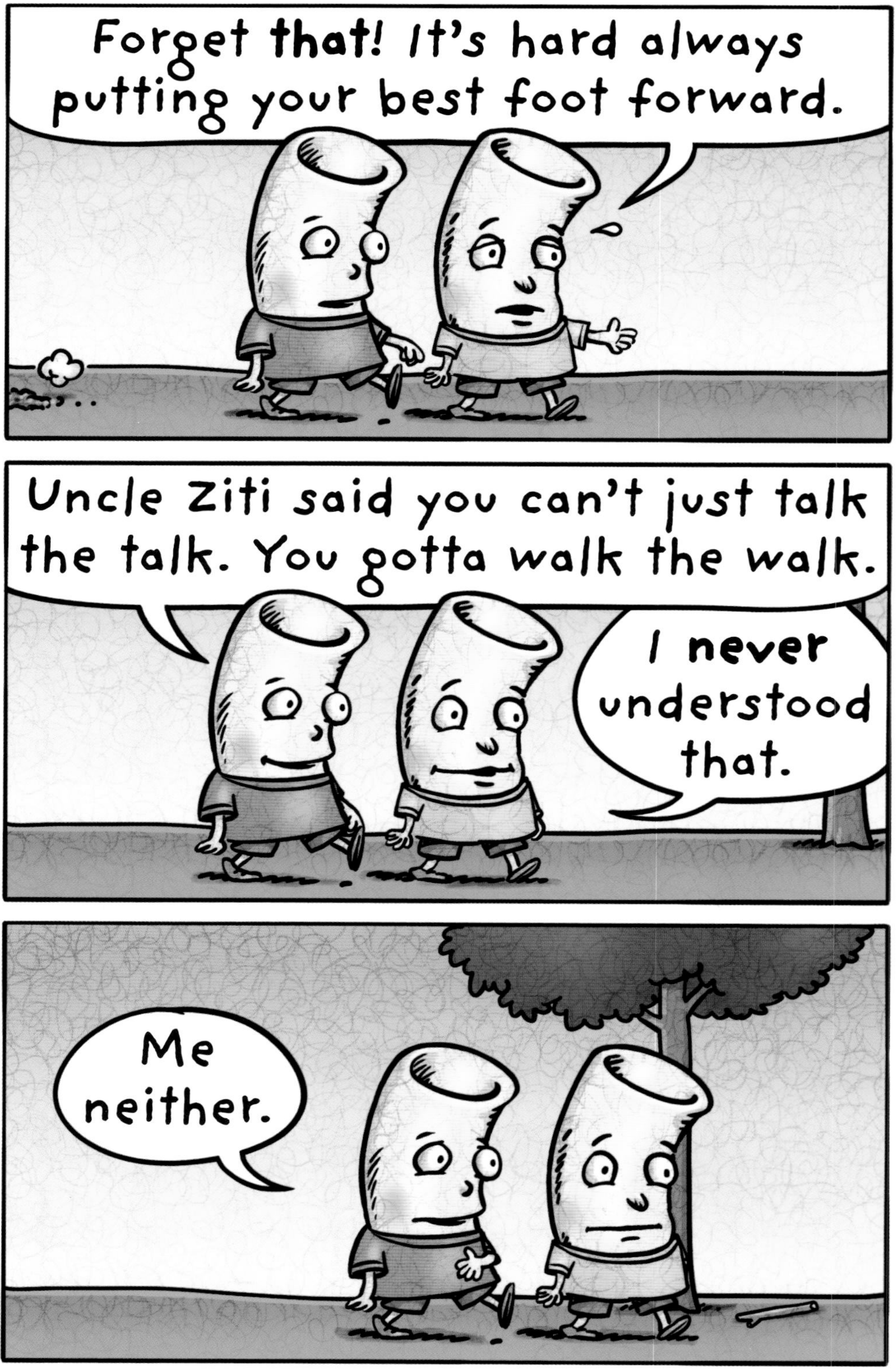
Forget that! It's hard always putting your best foot forward.
Uncle Ziti said you can't just talk the talk. You gotta walk the walk.
I never understood that.
Me neither.

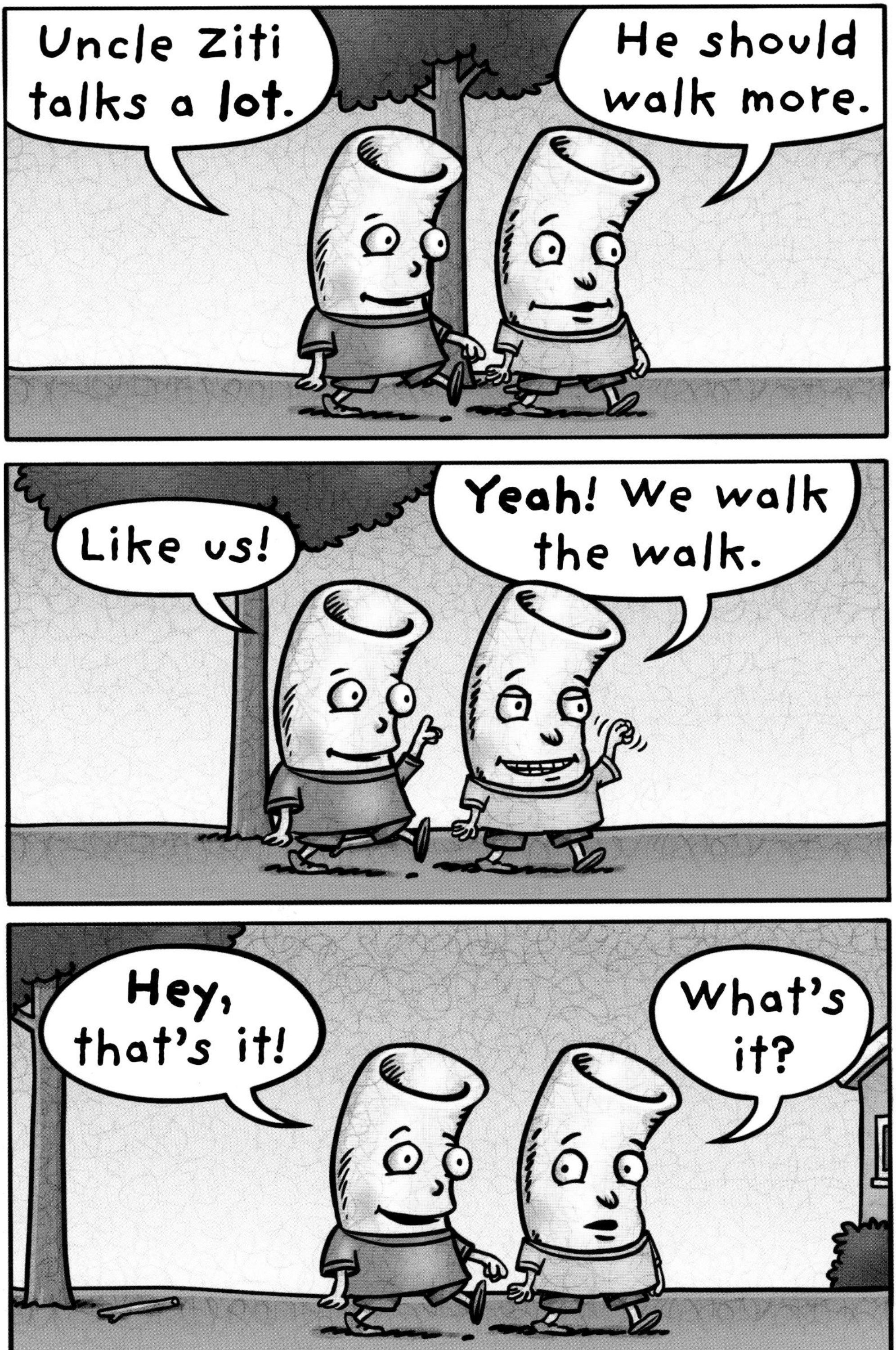
Uncle Ziti talks a lot.
He should walk more.
Like us!
Yeah! We walk the walk.
Hey, that's it!
What's it?

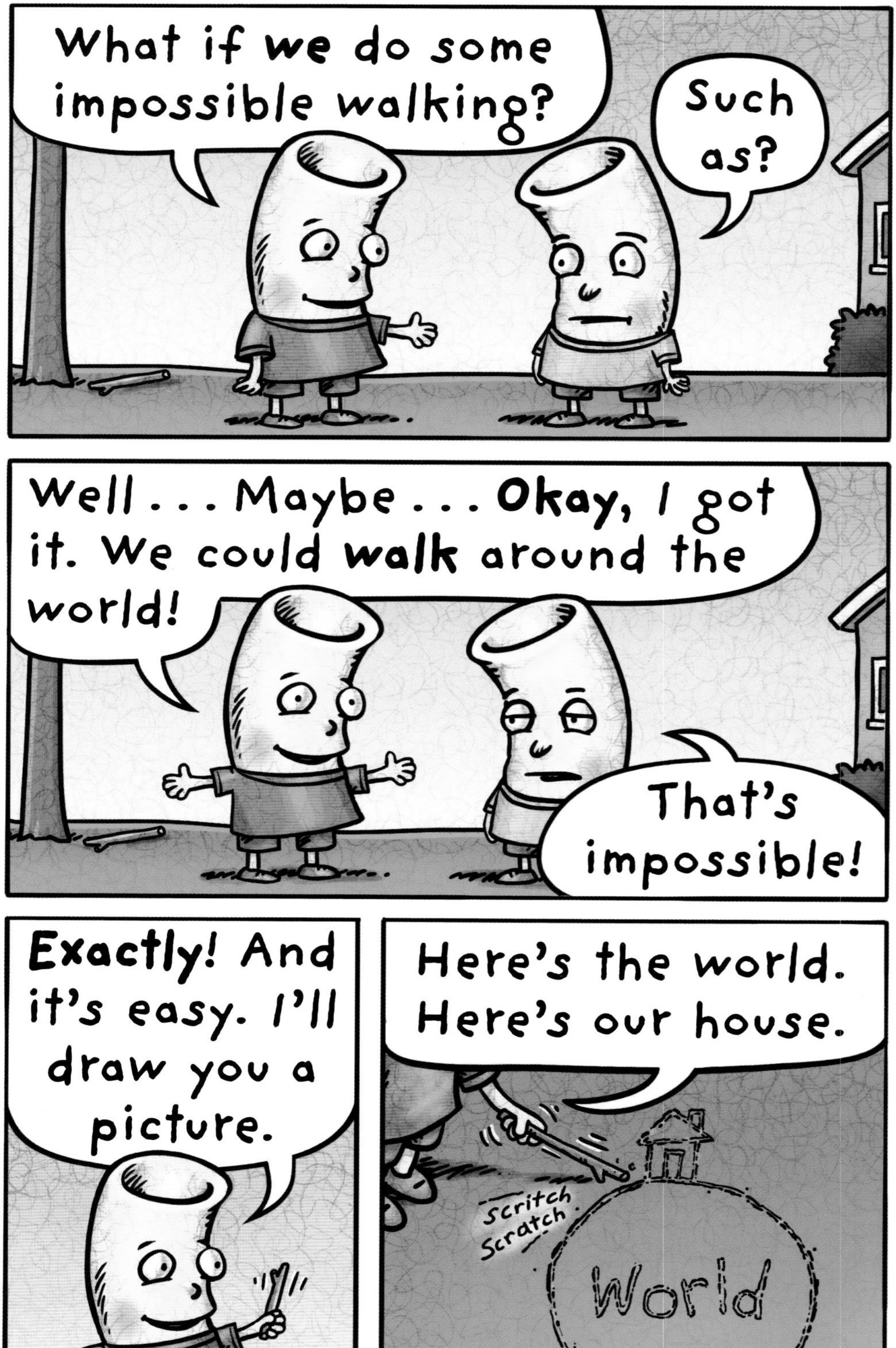
What if we do some impossible walking?
Such as?
Well . . . Maybe . . . Okay, I got it. We could walk around the world!
That's impossible!
Exactly! And it's easy. I'll draw you a picture.
Here's the world. Here's our house.
scritch scratch
World

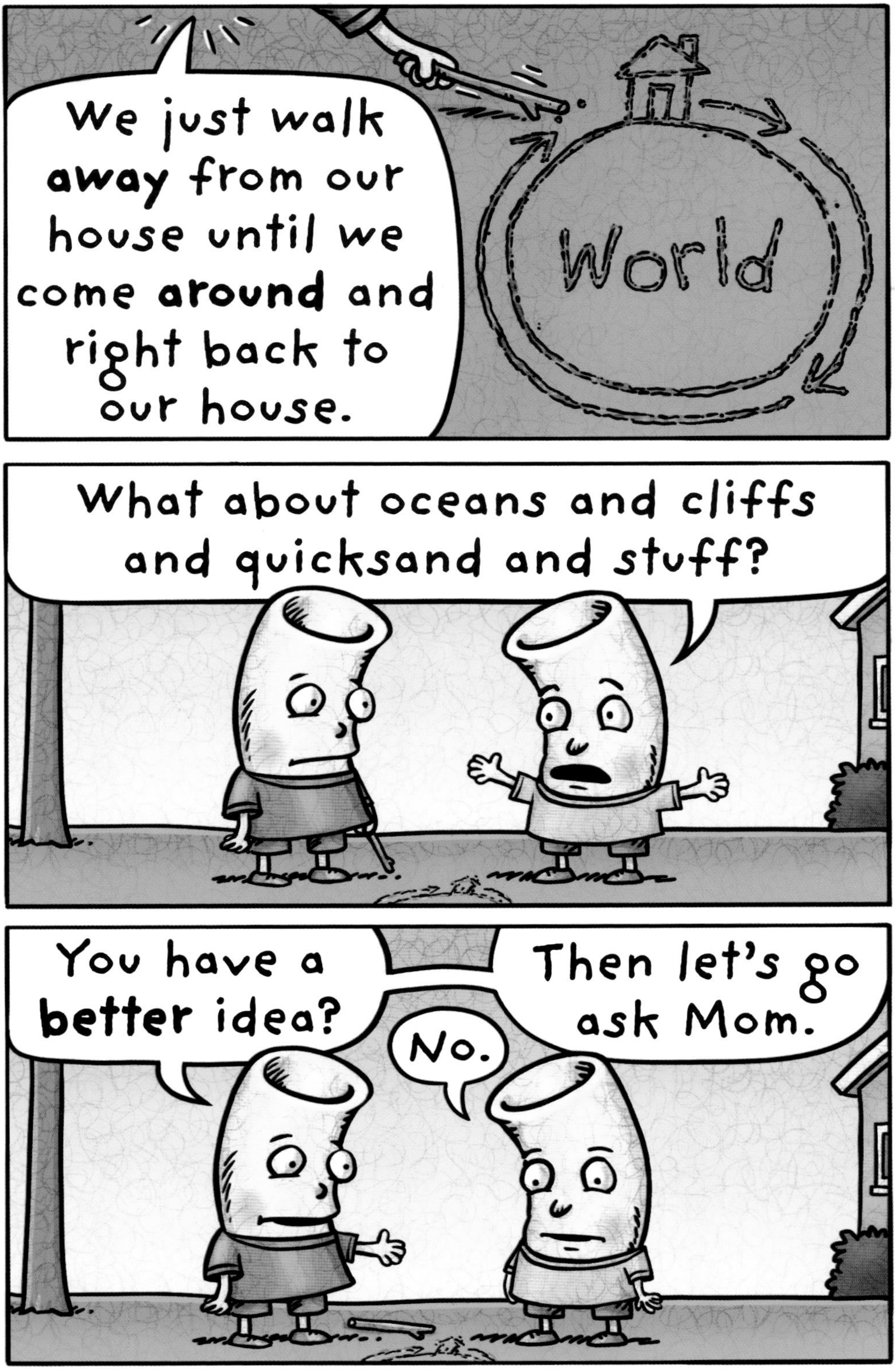
We just walk **away** from our house until we come **around** and right back to our house.
World
What about oceans and cliffs and quicksand and stuff?
You have a **better** idea?
No.
Then let's go ask Mom.

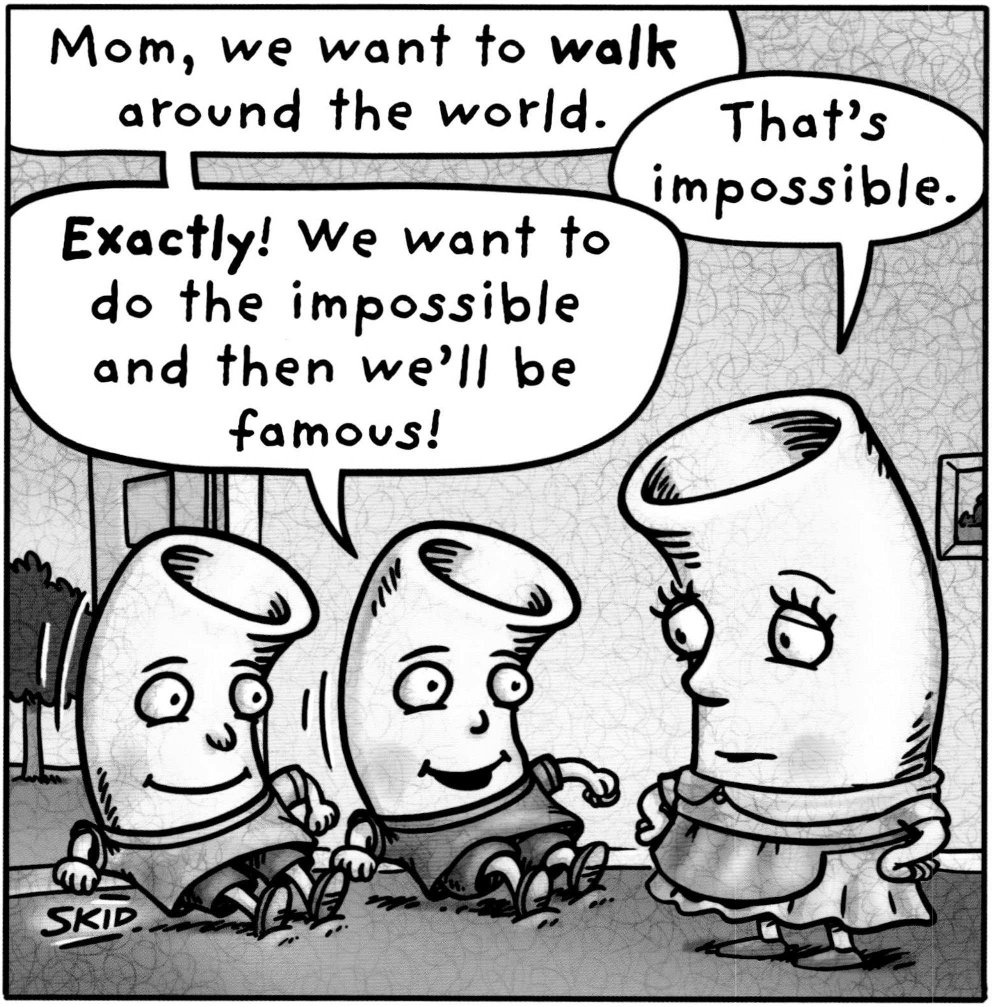
Mom, we want to **walk** around the world.
That's impossible.
Exactly! We want to do the impossible and then we'll be famous!
SKID

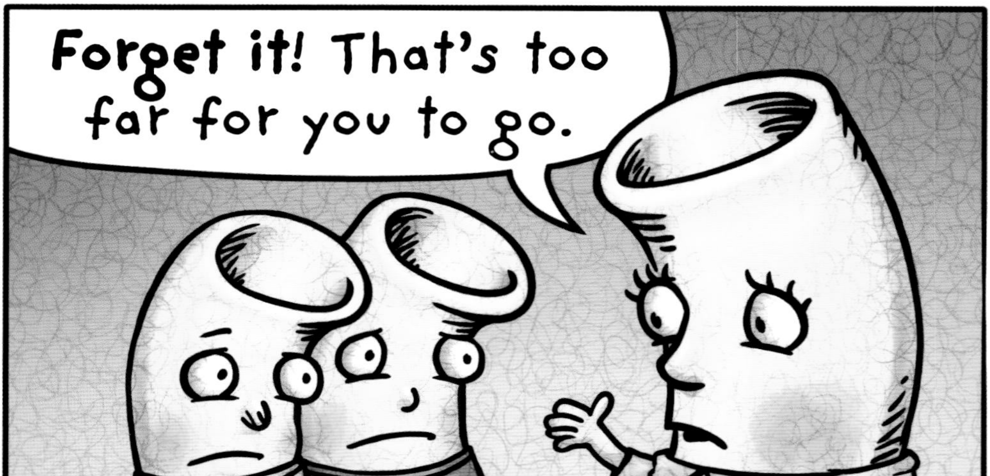
Forget it! That's too far for you to go.

NOODLEHEADS DO THE IMPOSSIBLE

CHAPTER 2
SEEING STARS

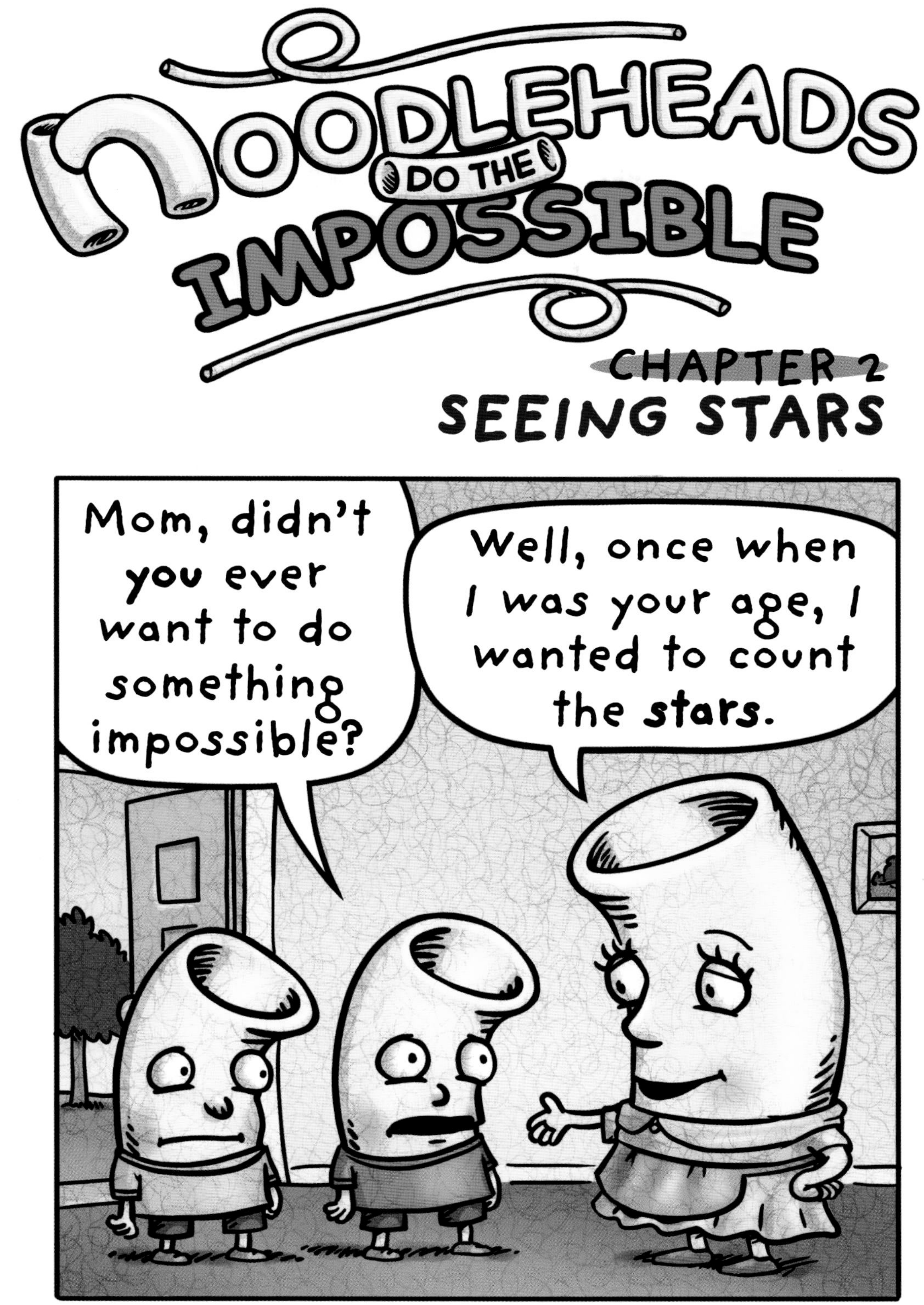

Mom, didn't you ever want to do something impossible?
Well, once when I was your age, I wanted to count the stars.

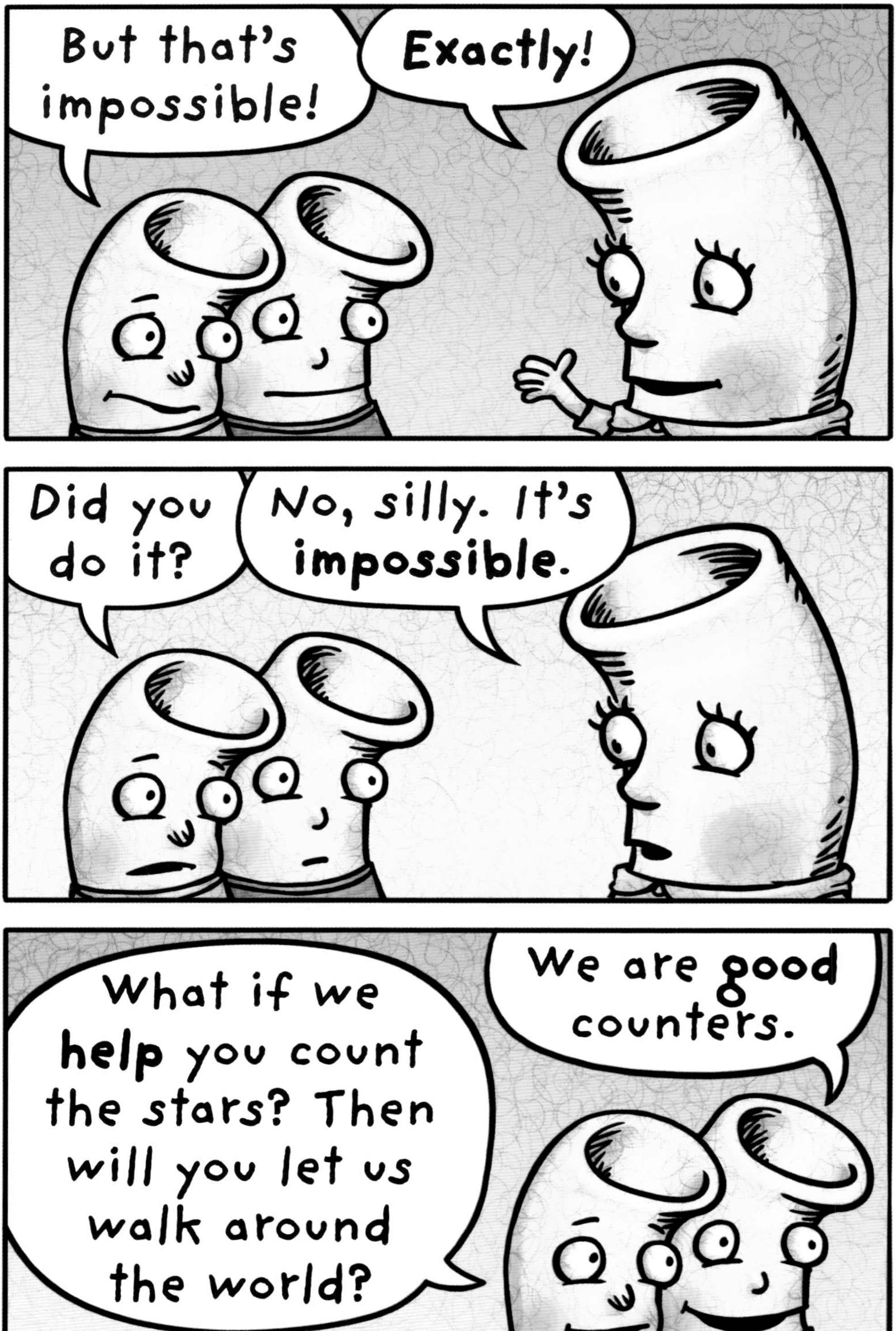
But that's impossible!
Exactly!
Did you do it?
No, silly. It's **impossible**.
What if we **help** you count the stars? Then will you let us walk around the world?
We are good counters.

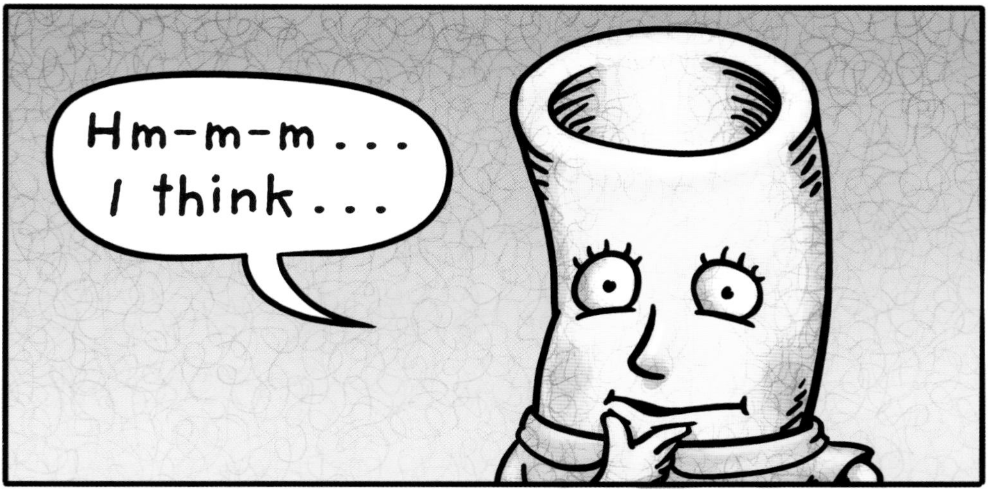
Hm-m-m . . .
I think . . .

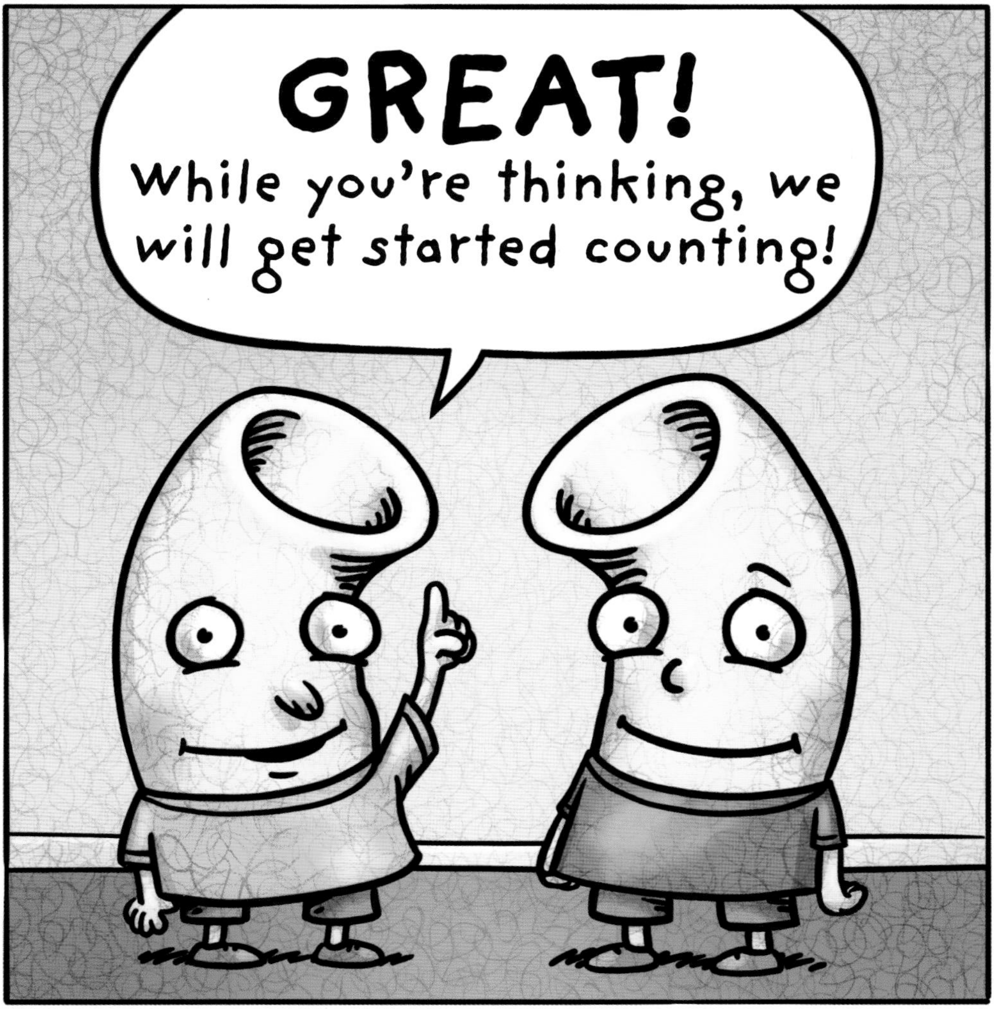
GREAT!
While you're thinking, we will get started counting!

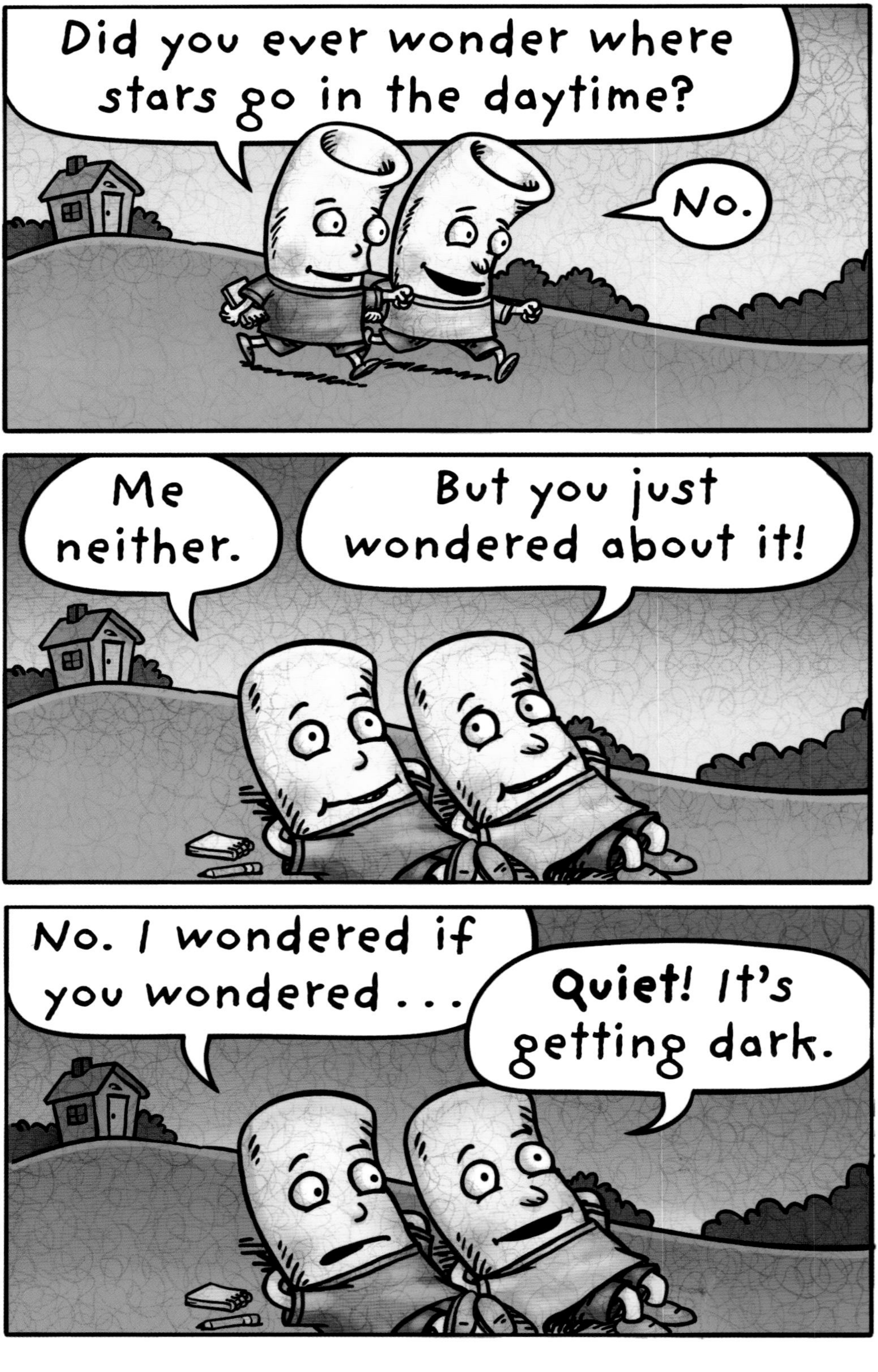
Did you ever wonder where stars go in the daytime?
No.
Me neither.
But you just wondered about it!
No. I wondered if you wondered . . .
Quiet! It's getting dark.

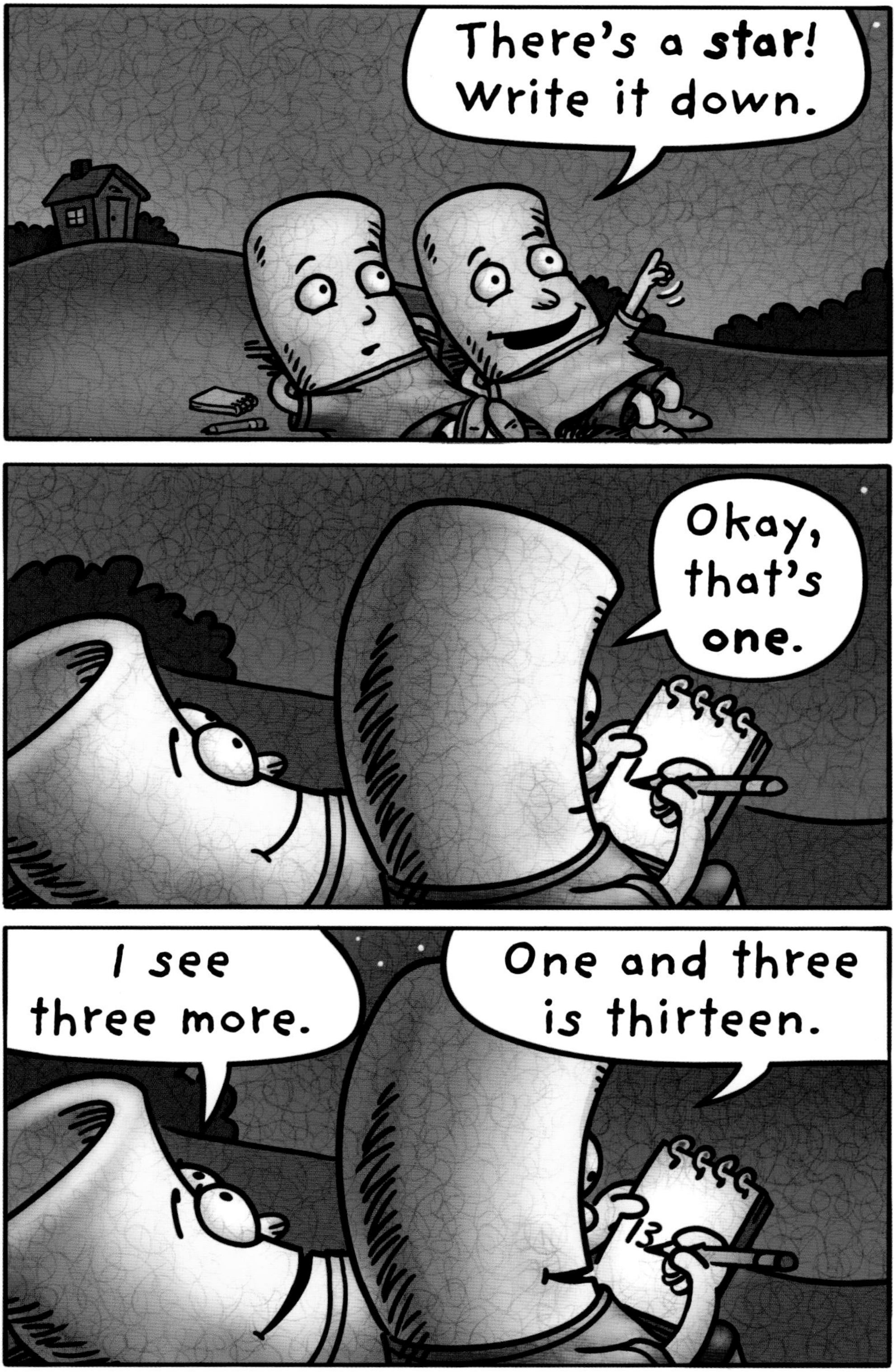
There's a star! Write it down.
Okay, that's one.
I see three more.
One and three is thirteen.
13

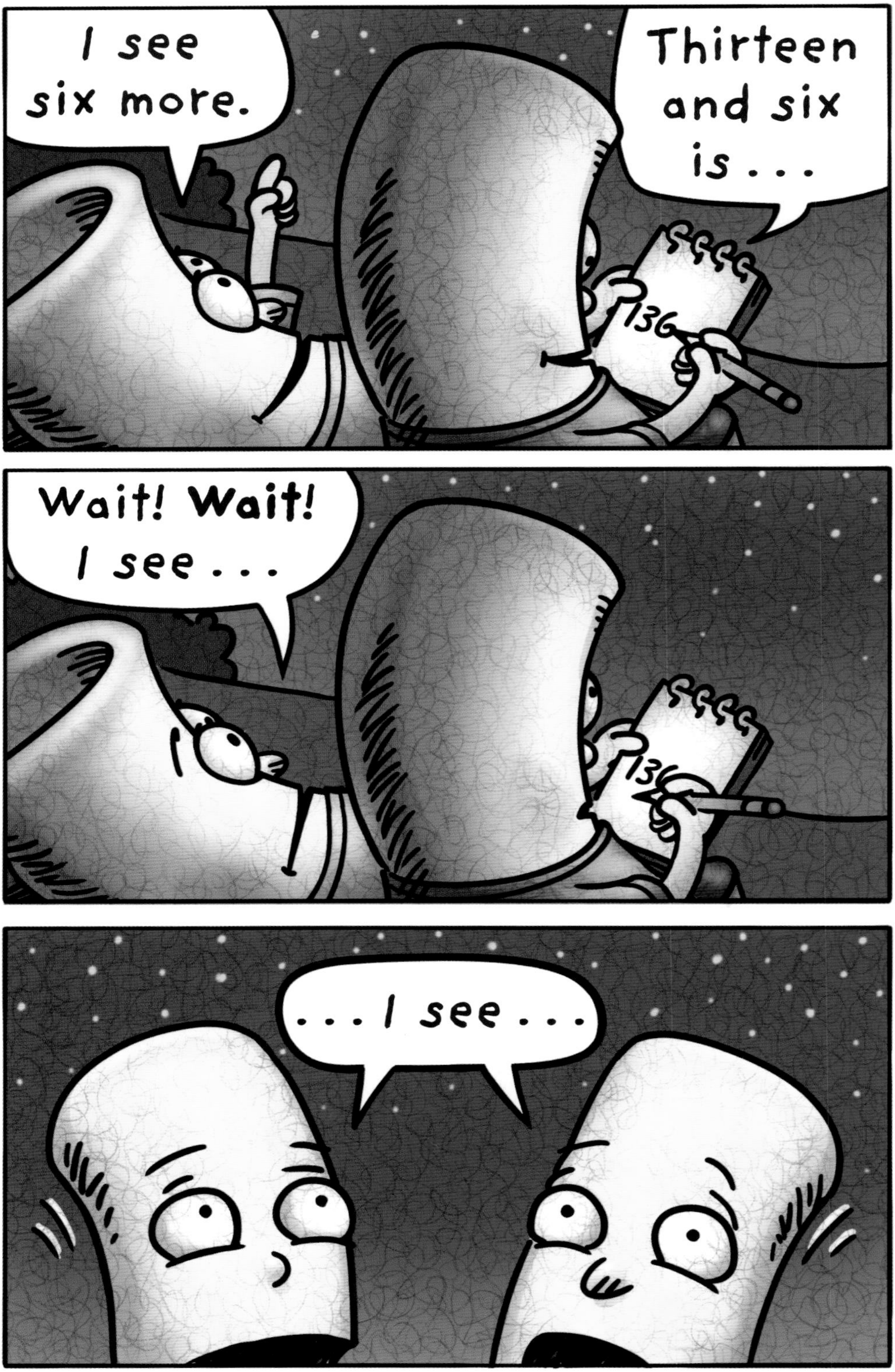
I see six more.
Thirteen and six is . . .
136
Wait! Wait! I see . . .
136
. . . I see . . .

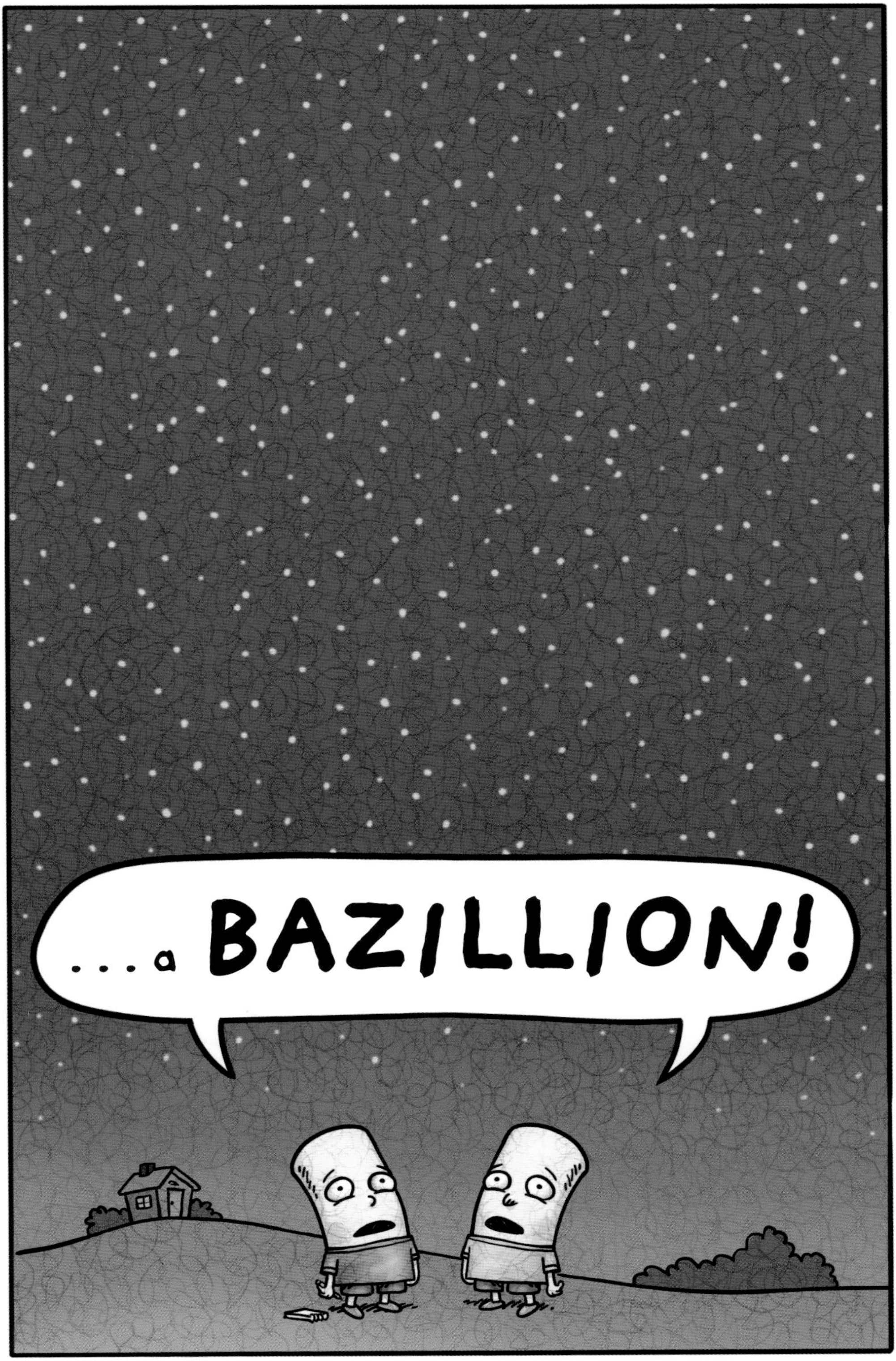
. . . a BAZILLION!

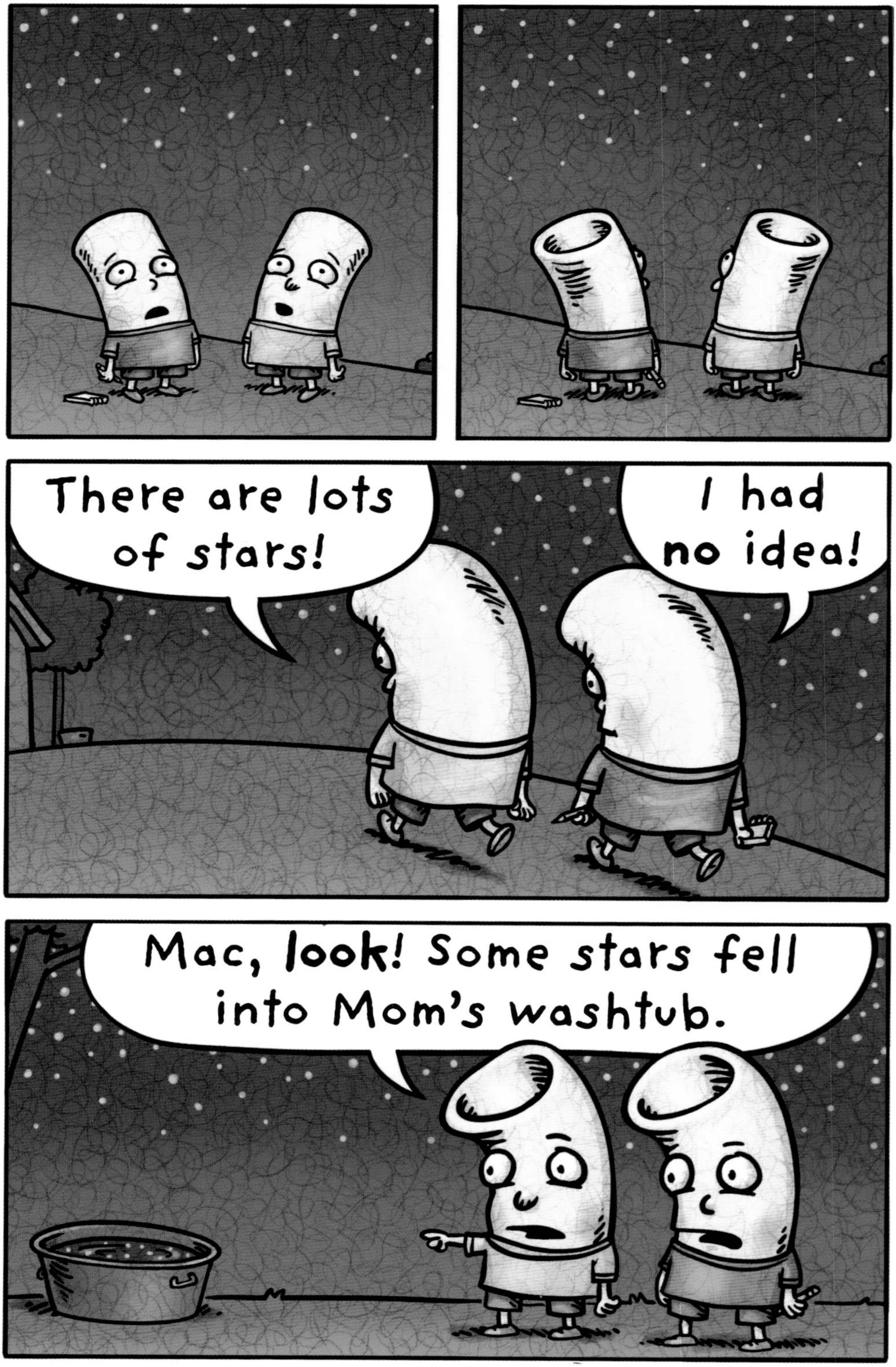
There are lots of stars!
I had no idea!
Mac, look! Some stars fell into Mom's washtub.

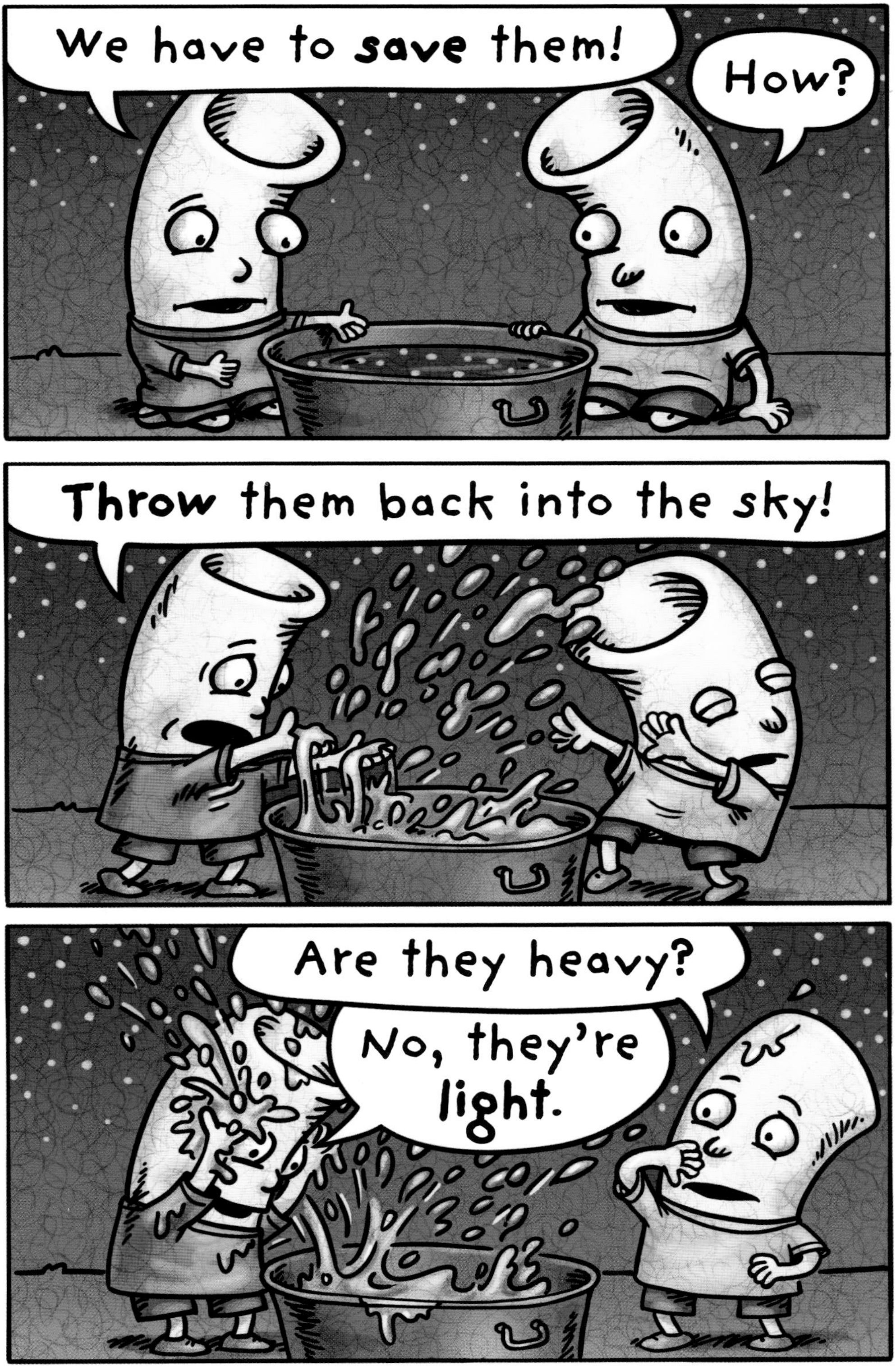
We have to save them!
How?
Throw them back into the sky!
Are they heavy?
No, they're light.

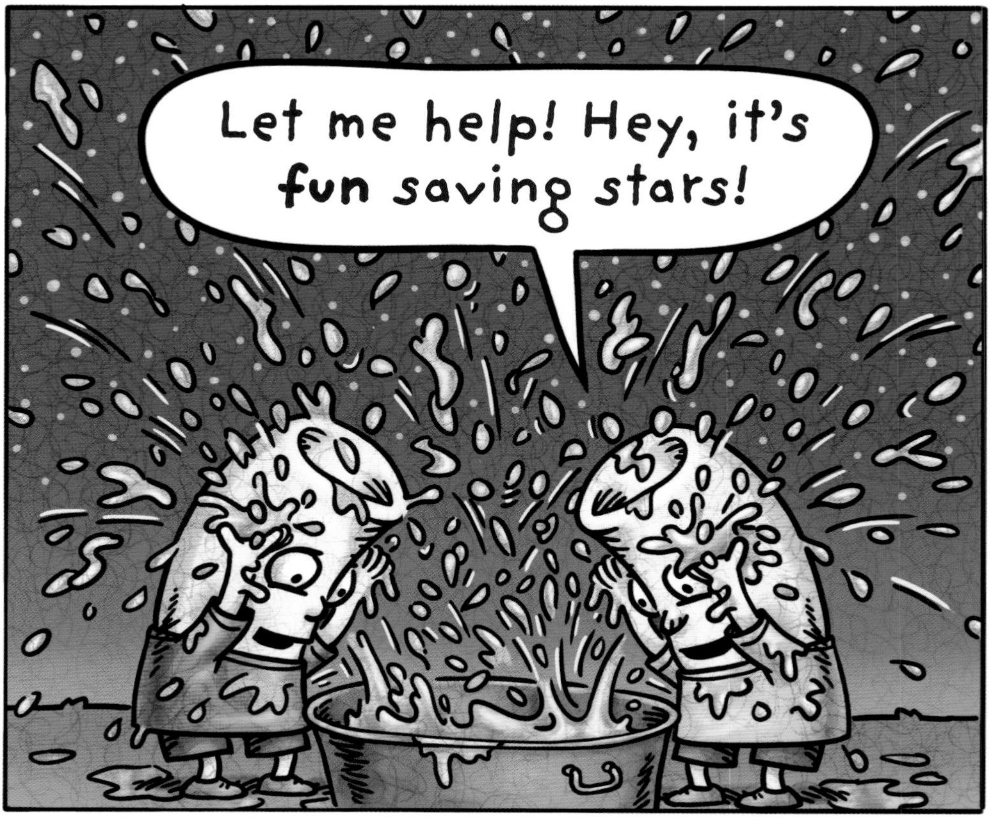
Let me help! Hey, it's **fun** saving stars!

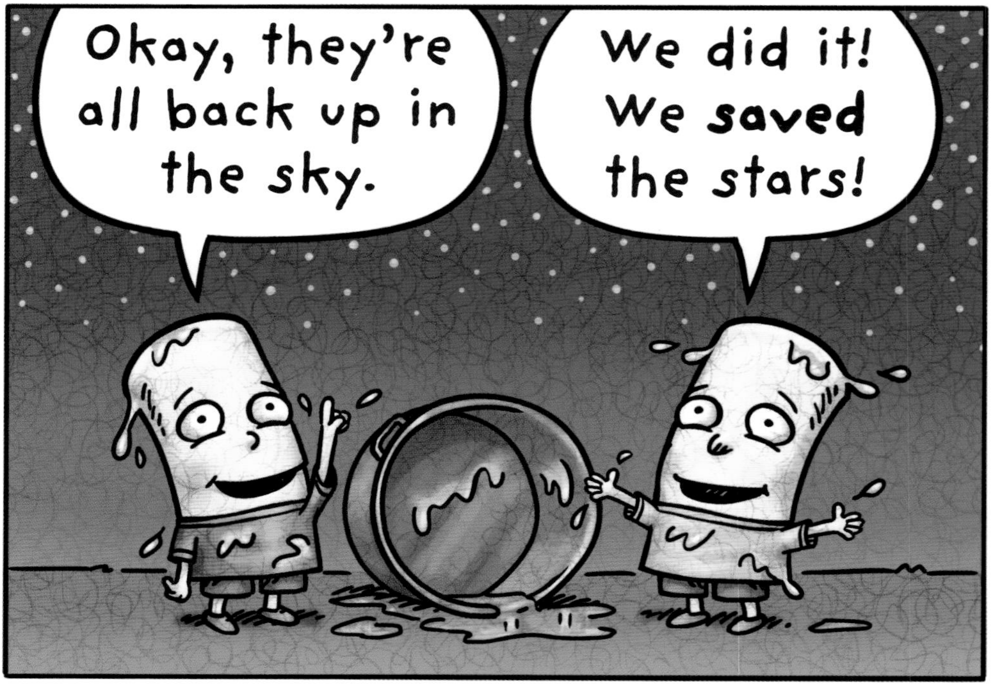
Okay, they're all back up in the sky.
We did it! We **saved** the stars!

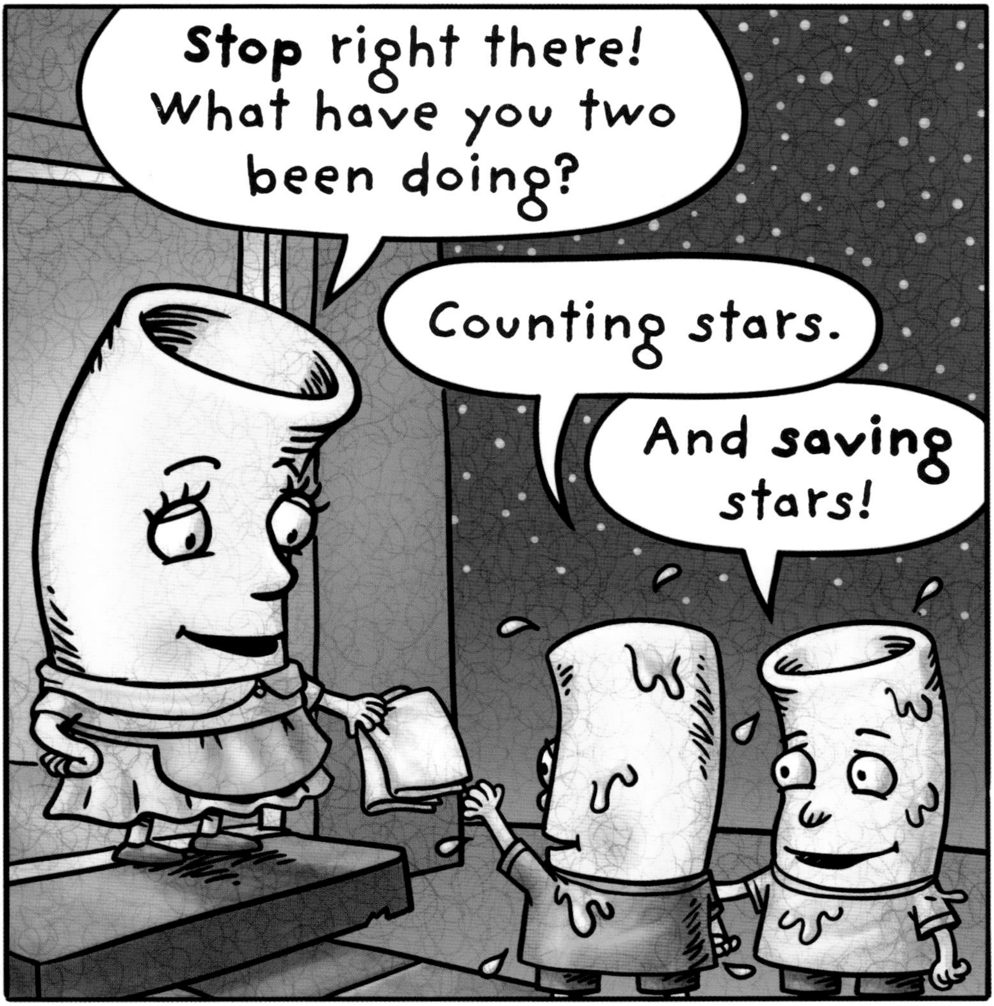
Stop right there! What have you two been doing?
Counting stars.
And saving stars!

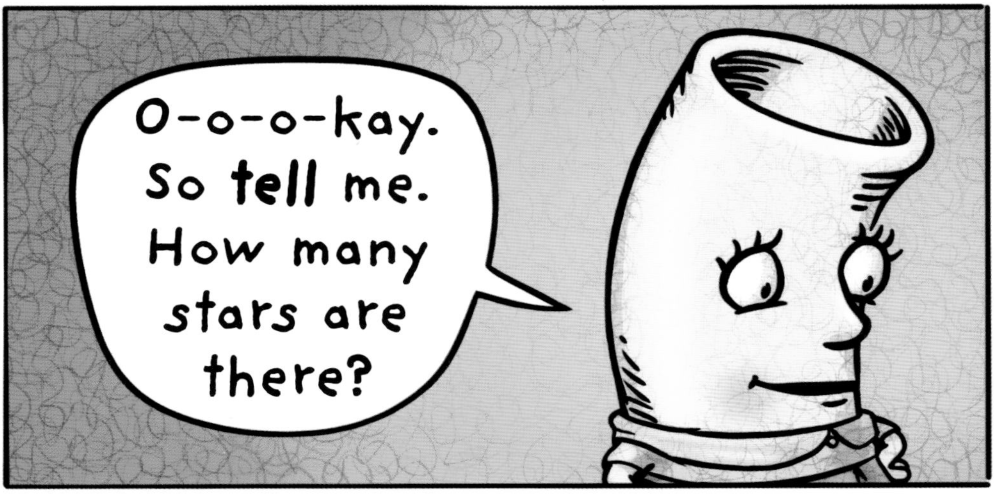
O-o-o-kay. So tell me. How many stars are there?

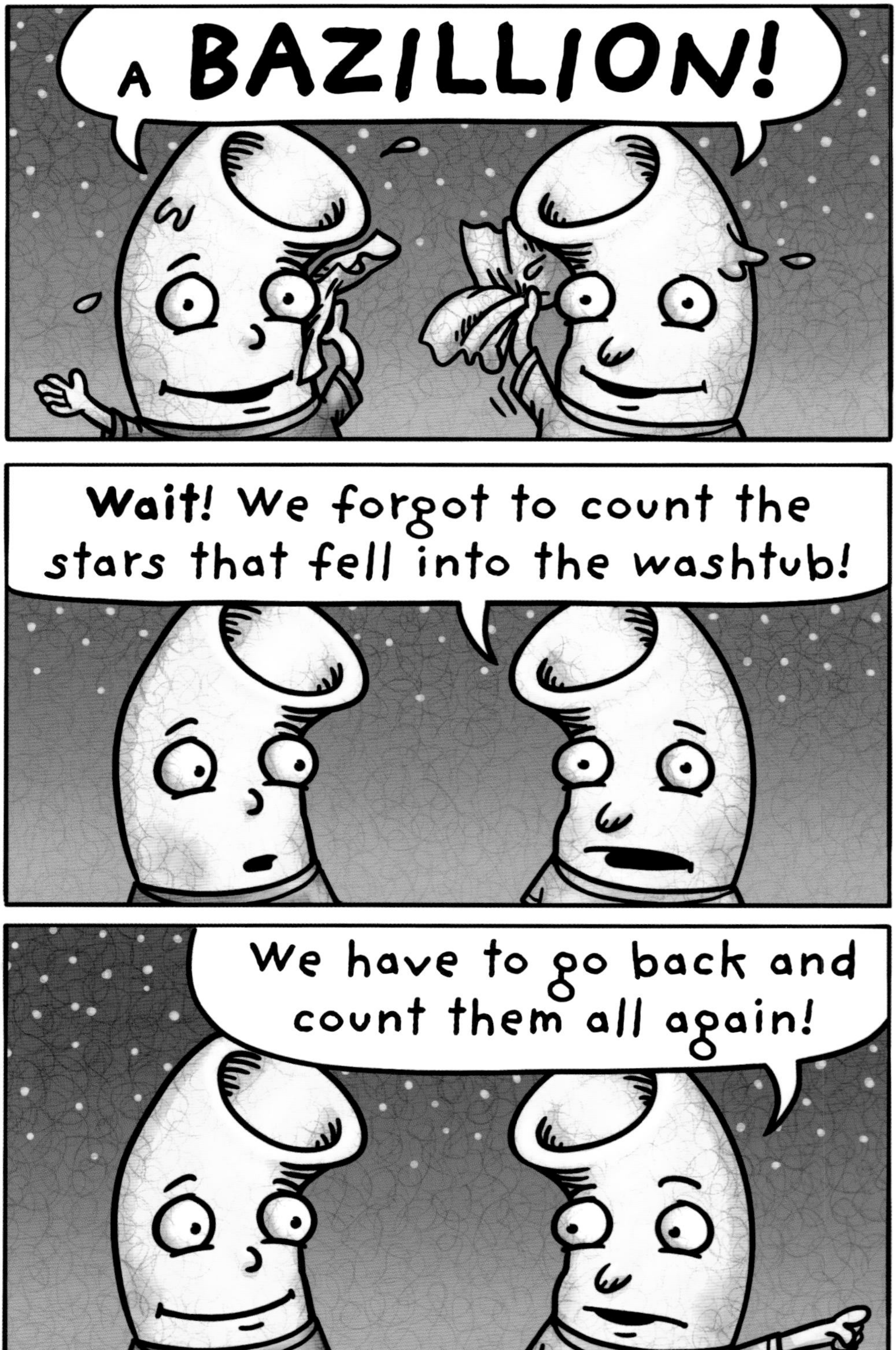
A BAZILLION!
Wait! We forgot to count the stars that fell into the washtub!
We have to go back and count them all again!

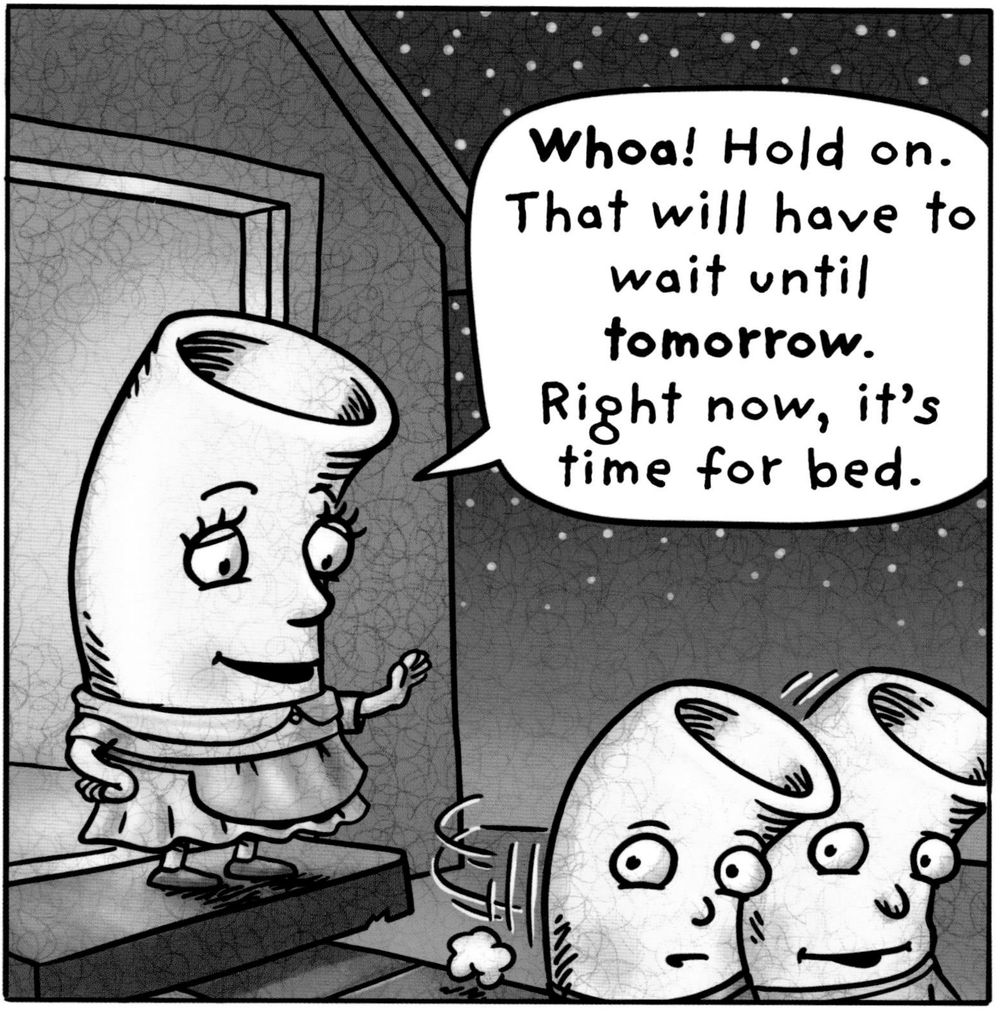
Whoa! Hold on. That will have to wait until **tomorrow.** Right now, it's time for bed.

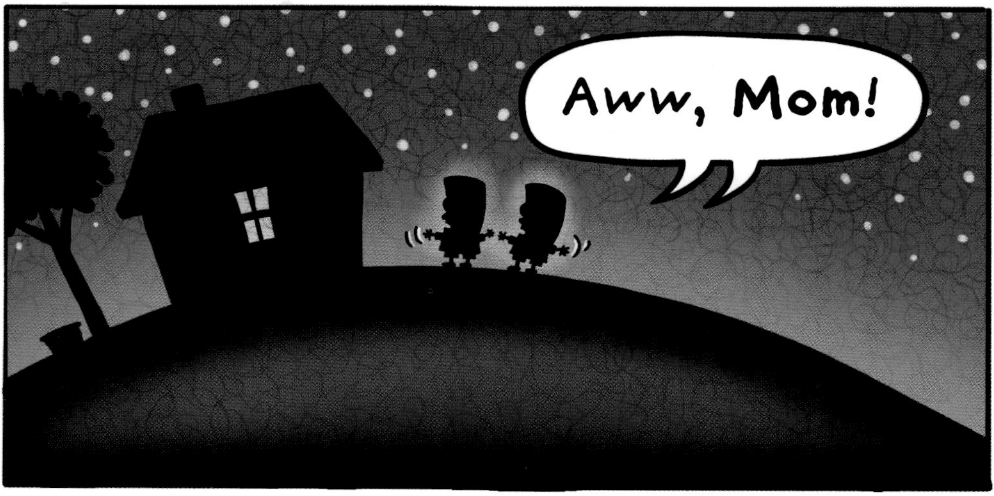
Aww, Mom!

NOODLEHEADS DO THE IMPOSSIBLE

CHAPTER 3
FOLLOW YOUR SHOES

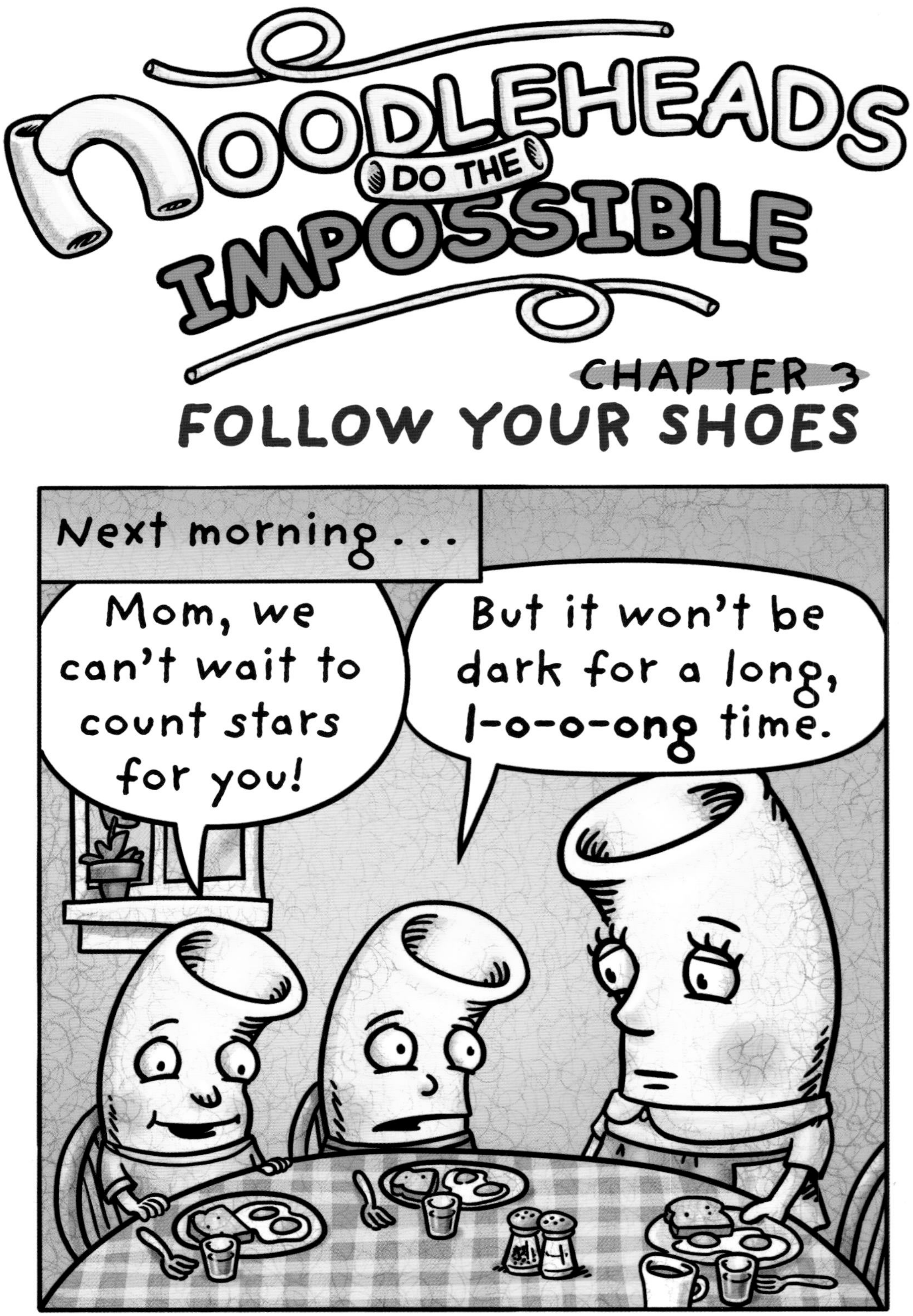

Next morning . . .
Mom, we can't wait to count stars for you!
But it won't be dark for a long, l-o-o-ong time.

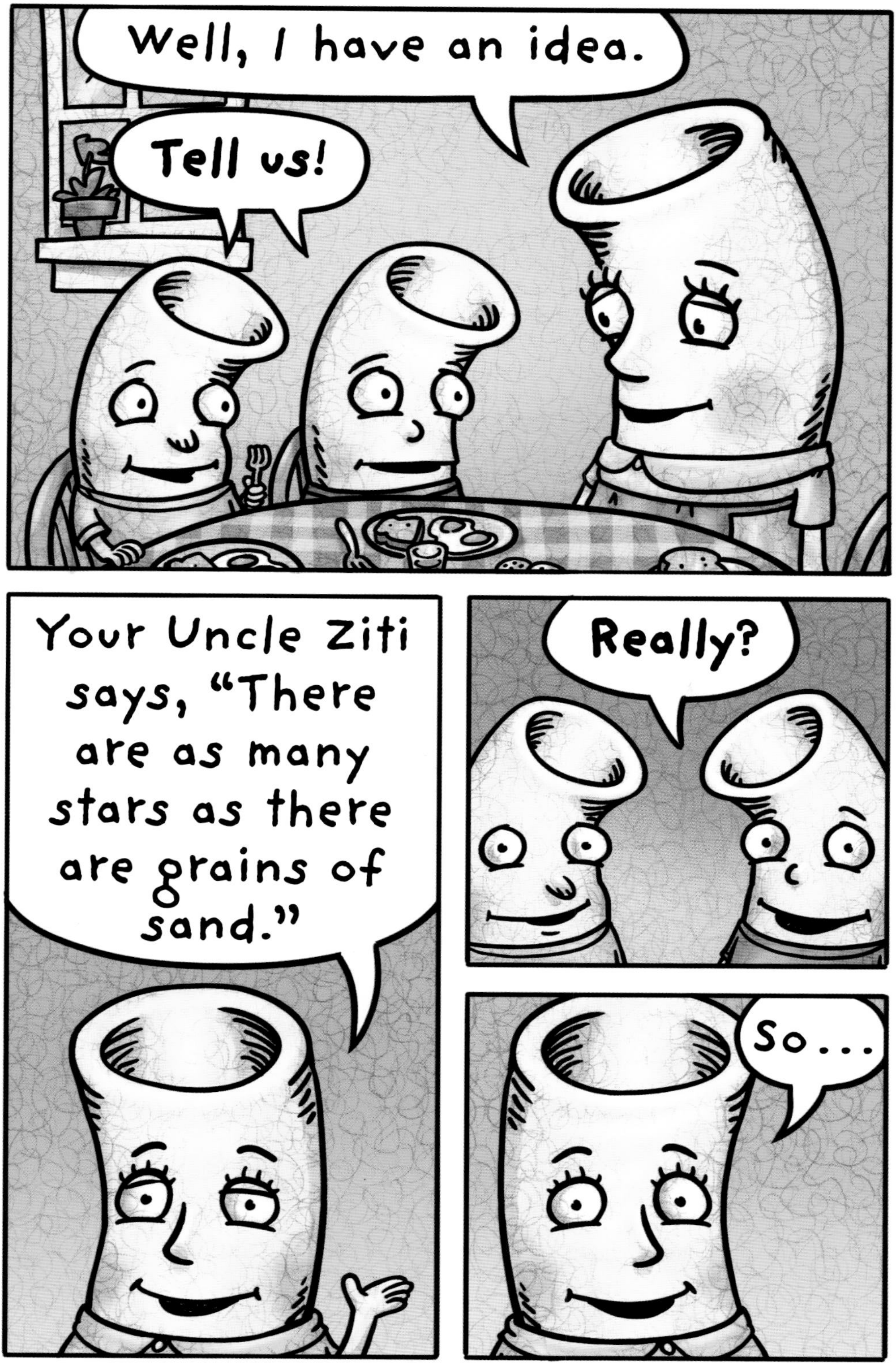
Well, I have an idea.
Tell us!
Your Uncle Ziti says, "There are as many stars as there are grains of sand."
Really?
So...

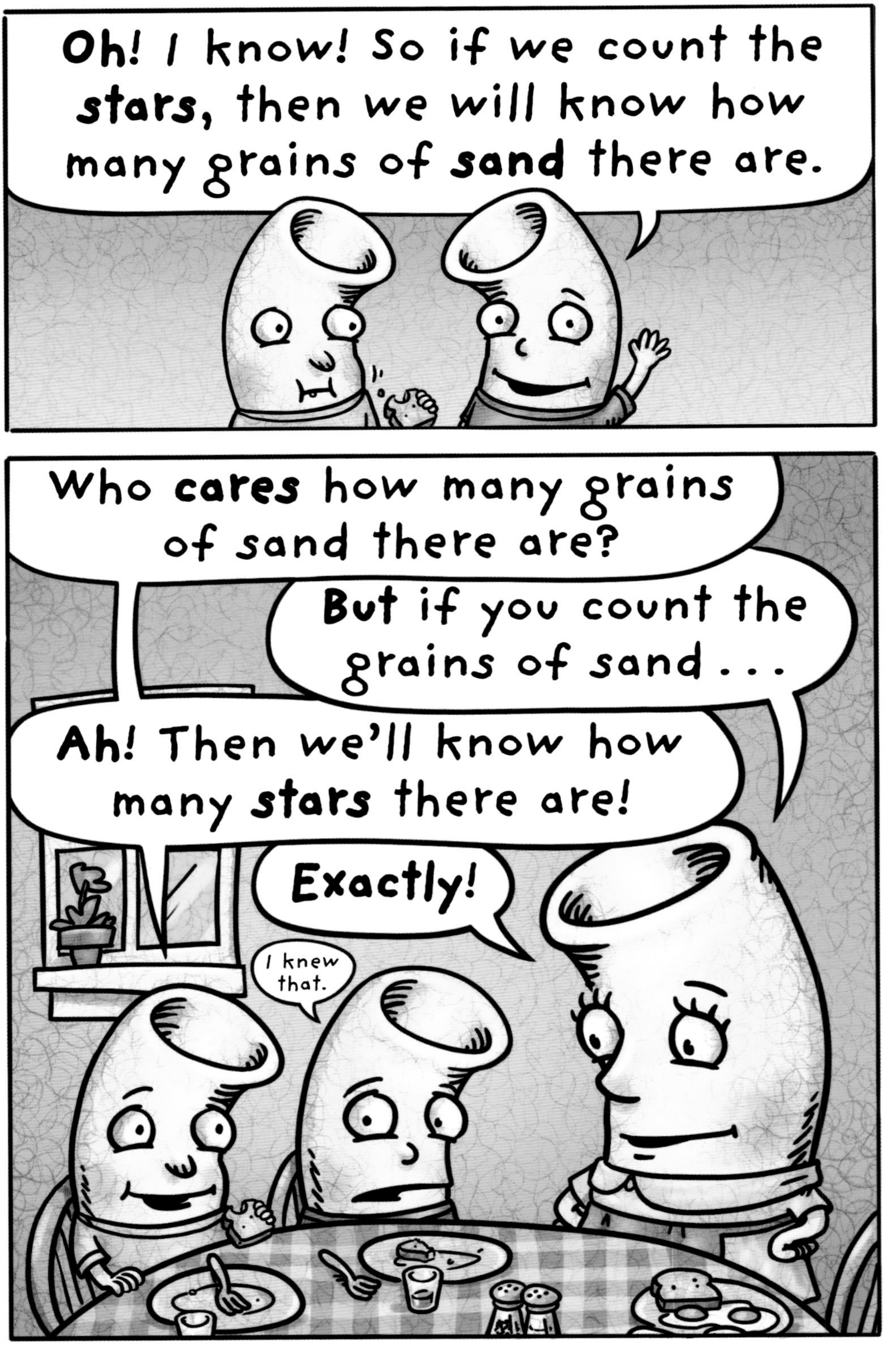
Oh! I know! So if we count the stars, then we will know how many grains of sand there are.
Who cares how many grains of sand there are?
But if you count the grains of sand . . .
Ah! Then we'll know how many stars there are!
Exactly!
I knew that.

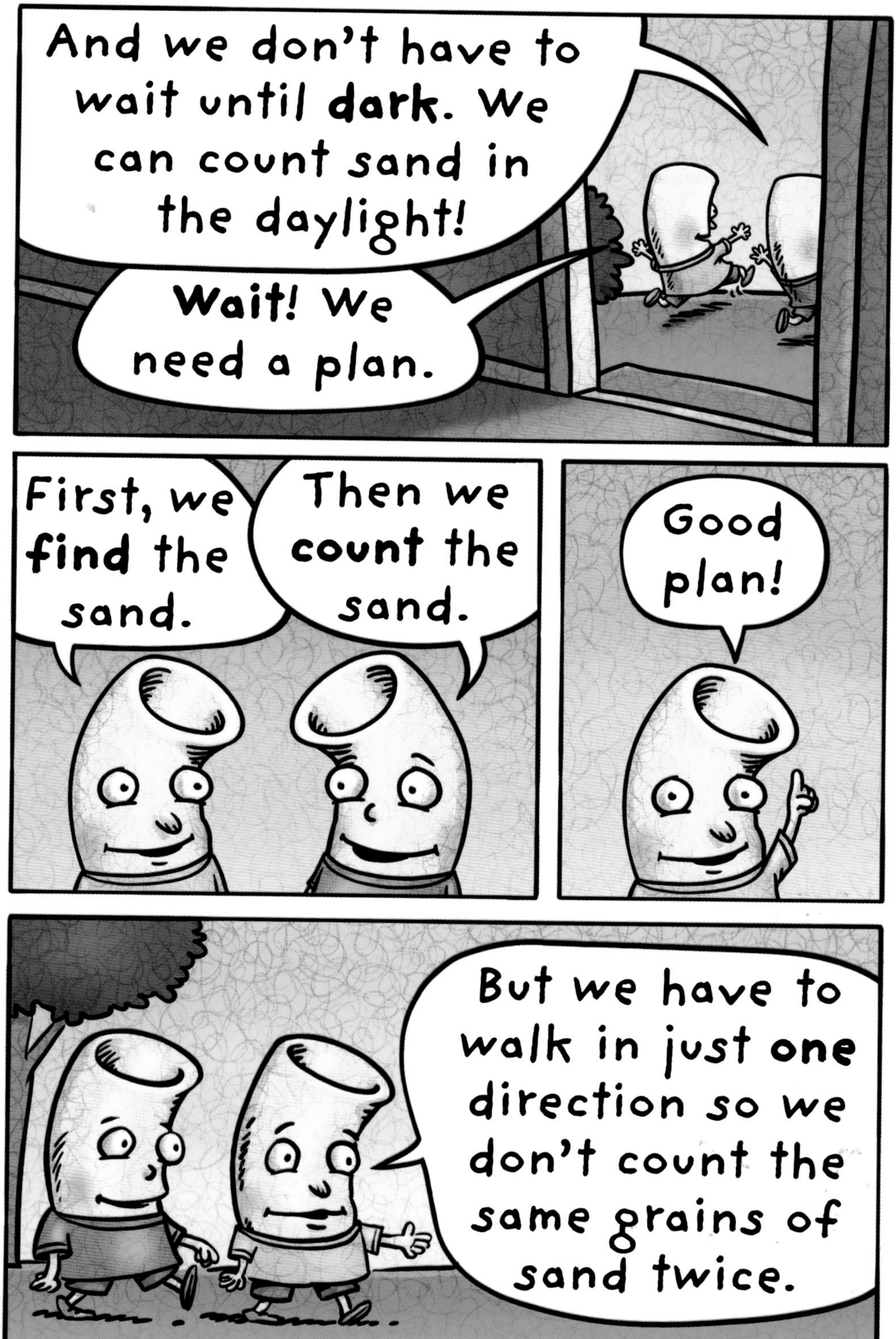
And we don't have to wait until **dark**. We can count sand in the daylight!
Wait! We need a plan.
First, we **find** the sand.
Then we **count** the sand.
Good plan!
But we have to walk in just **one** direction so we don't count the same grains of sand twice.

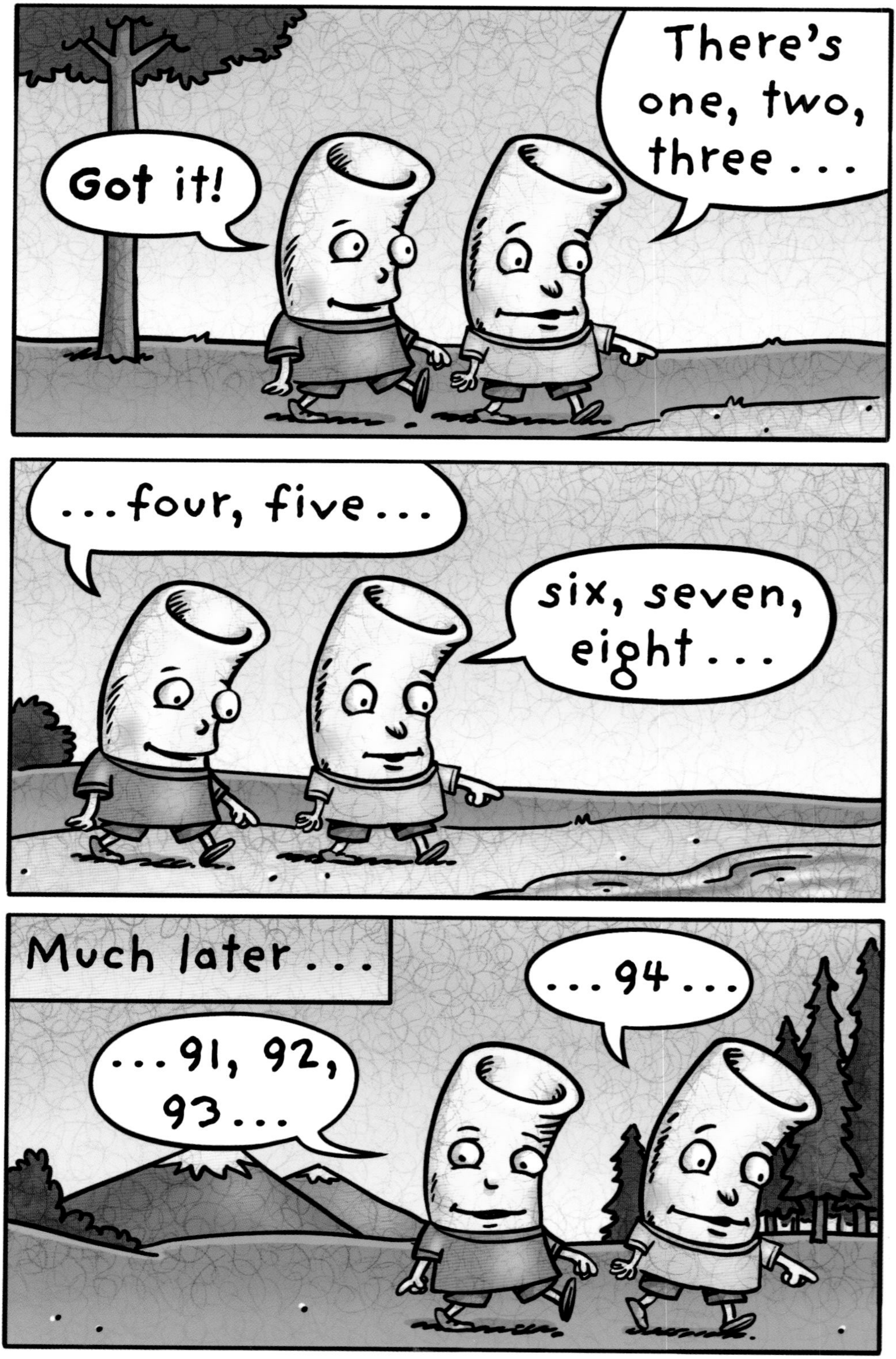

Got it!
There's one, two, three . . .
. . . four, five . . .
six, seven, eight . . .
Much later . . .
. . . 91, 92, 93 . . .
. . . 94 . . .

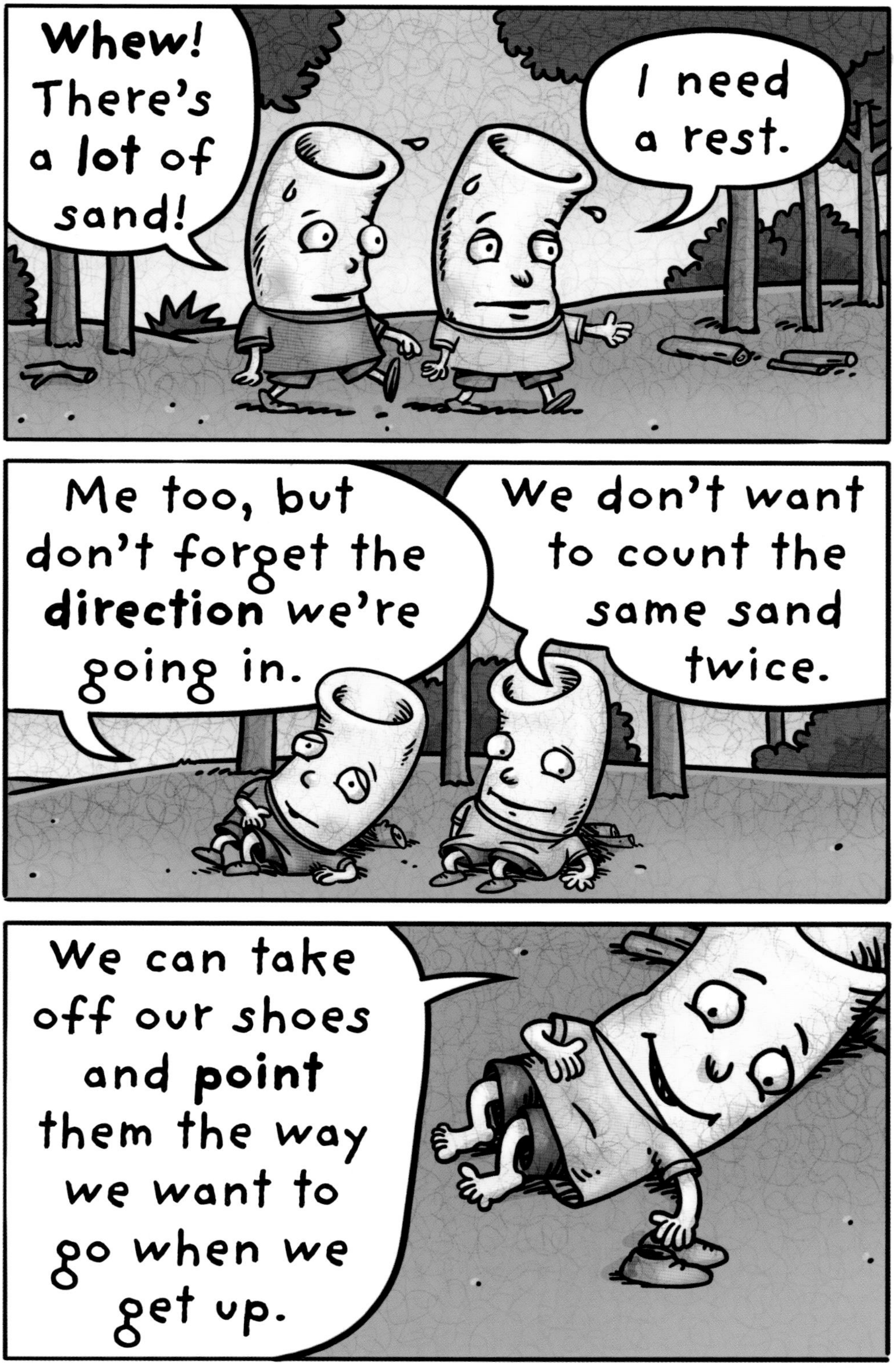
Whew! There's a **lot** of sand!
I need a rest.
Me too, but don't forget the **direction** we're going in.
We don't want to count the same sand twice.
We can take off our shoes and **point** them the way we want to go when we get up.

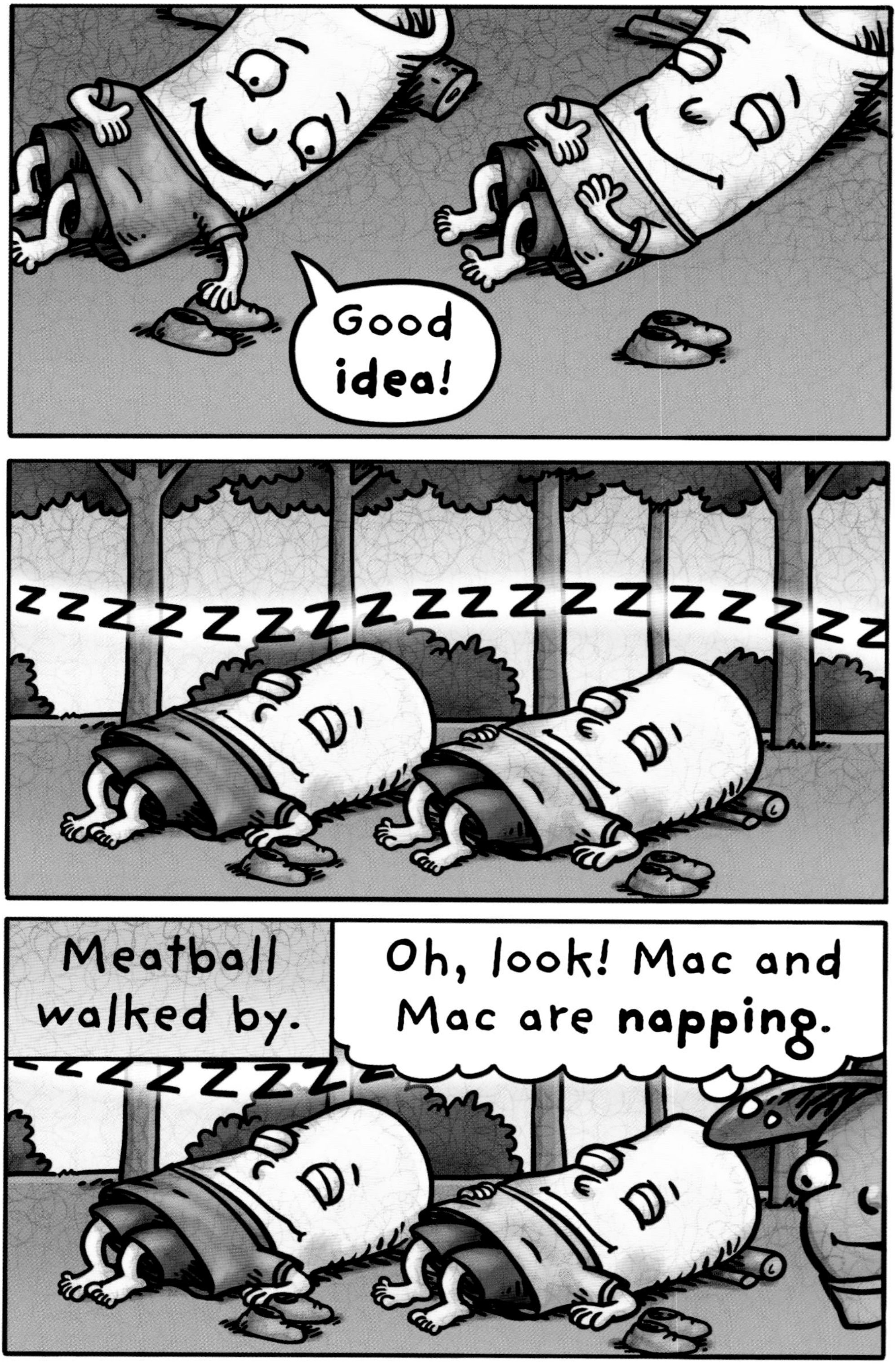
Good idea!
ZZZZZZZZZZZZZZZZZZZ
Meatball walked by.
Oh, look! Mac and Mac are napping.
ZZZZZZ

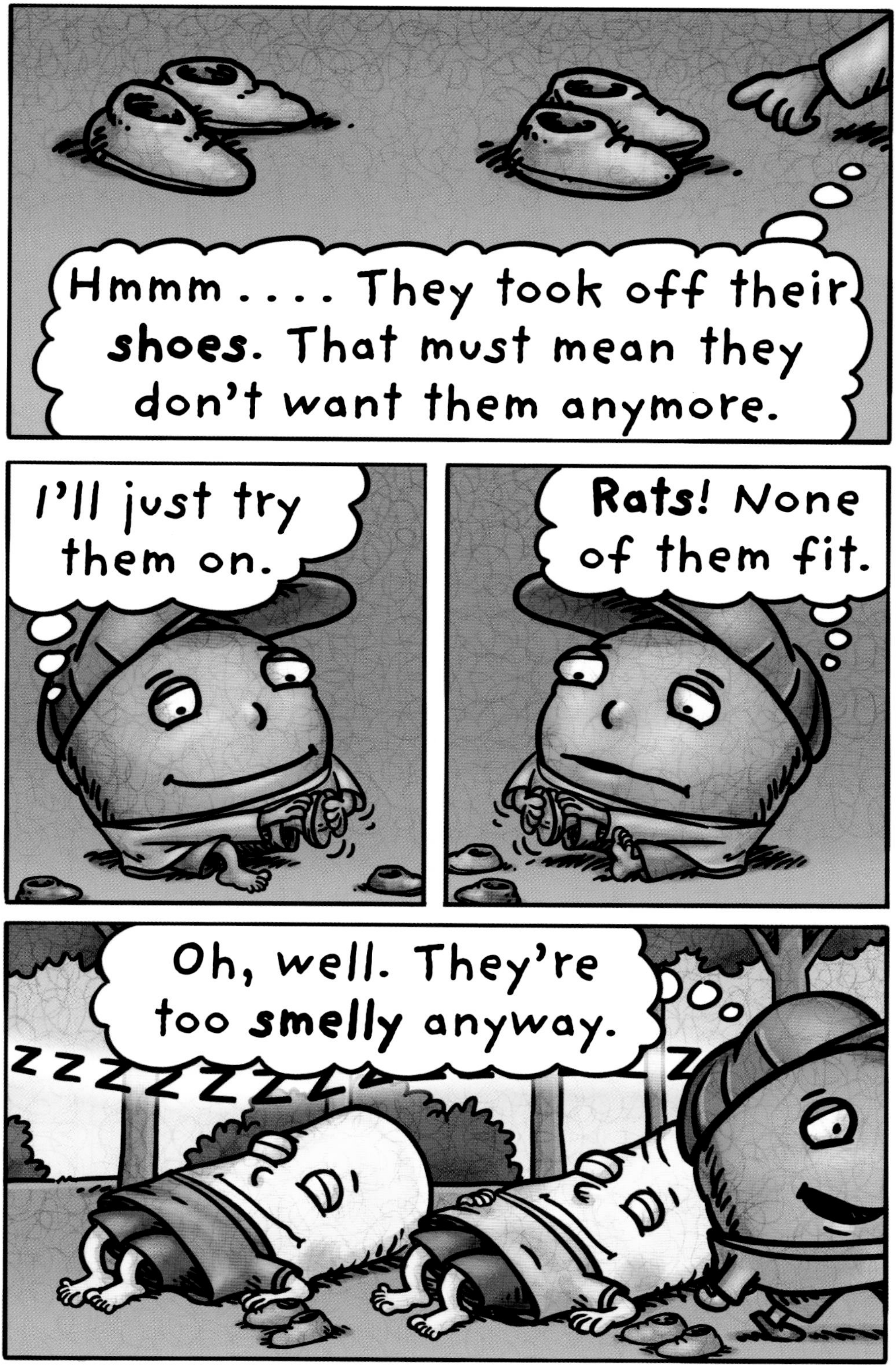
Hmmm . . . . They took off their shoes. That must mean they don't want them anymore.
I'll just try them on.
Rats! None of them fit.
Oh, well. They're too smelly anyway.
ZZZZZZZZZ

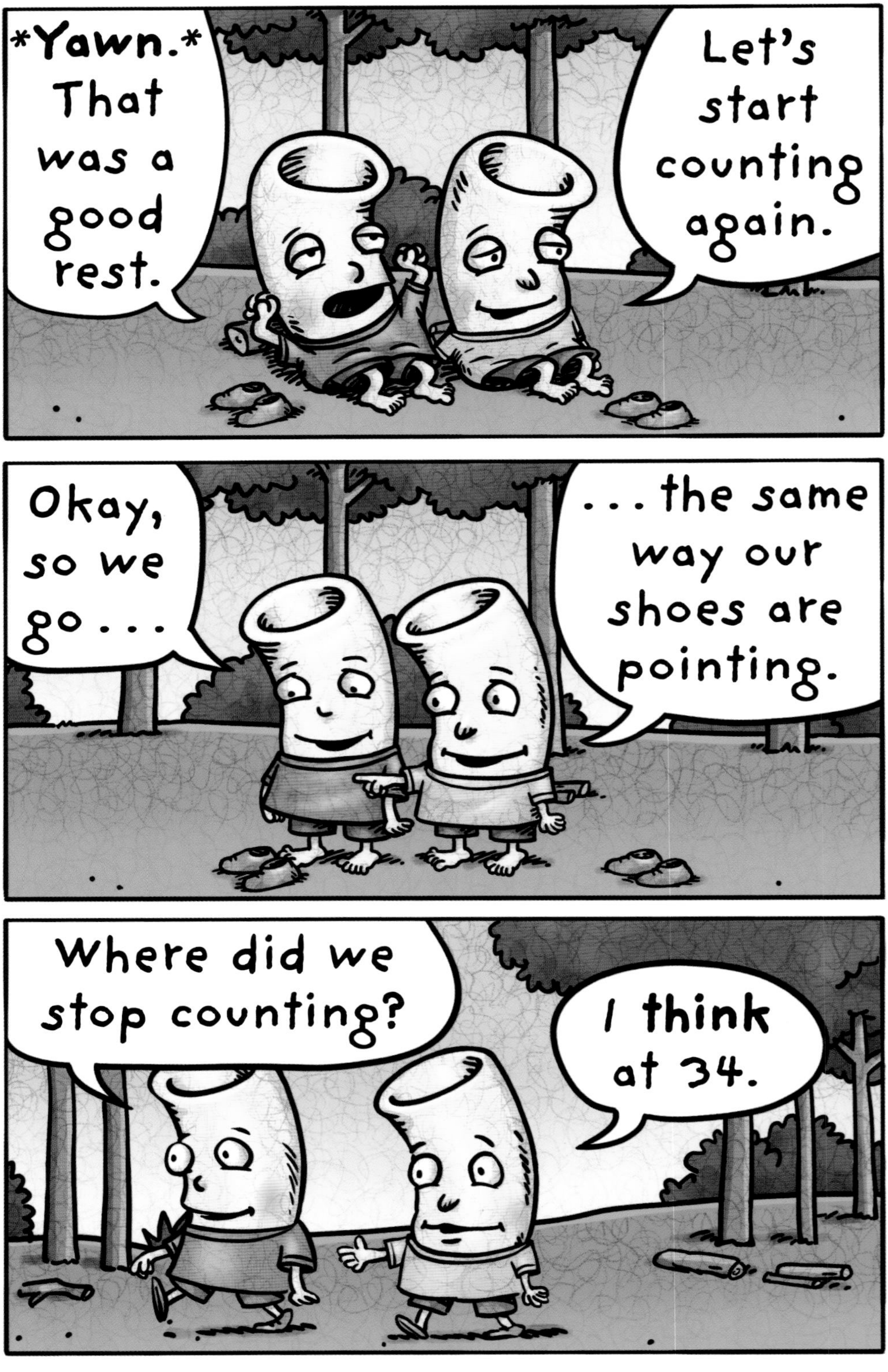
Yawn. That was a good rest.
Let's start counting again.
Okay, so we go . . .
. . . the same way our shoes are pointing.
Where did we stop counting?
I think at 34.

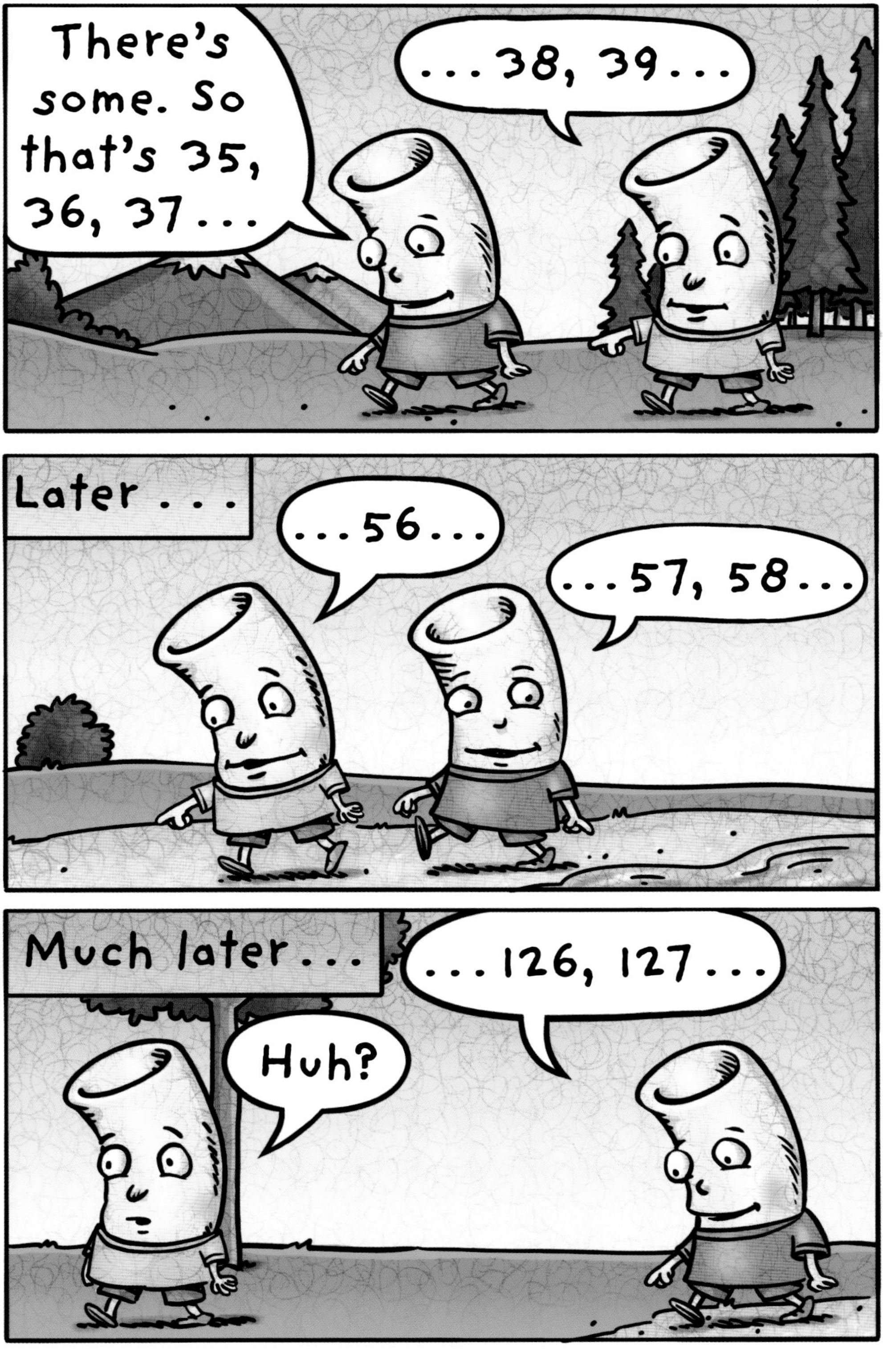
There's some. So that's 35, 36, 37...
...38, 39...
Later...
...56...
...57, 58...
Much later...
...126, 127...
Huh?

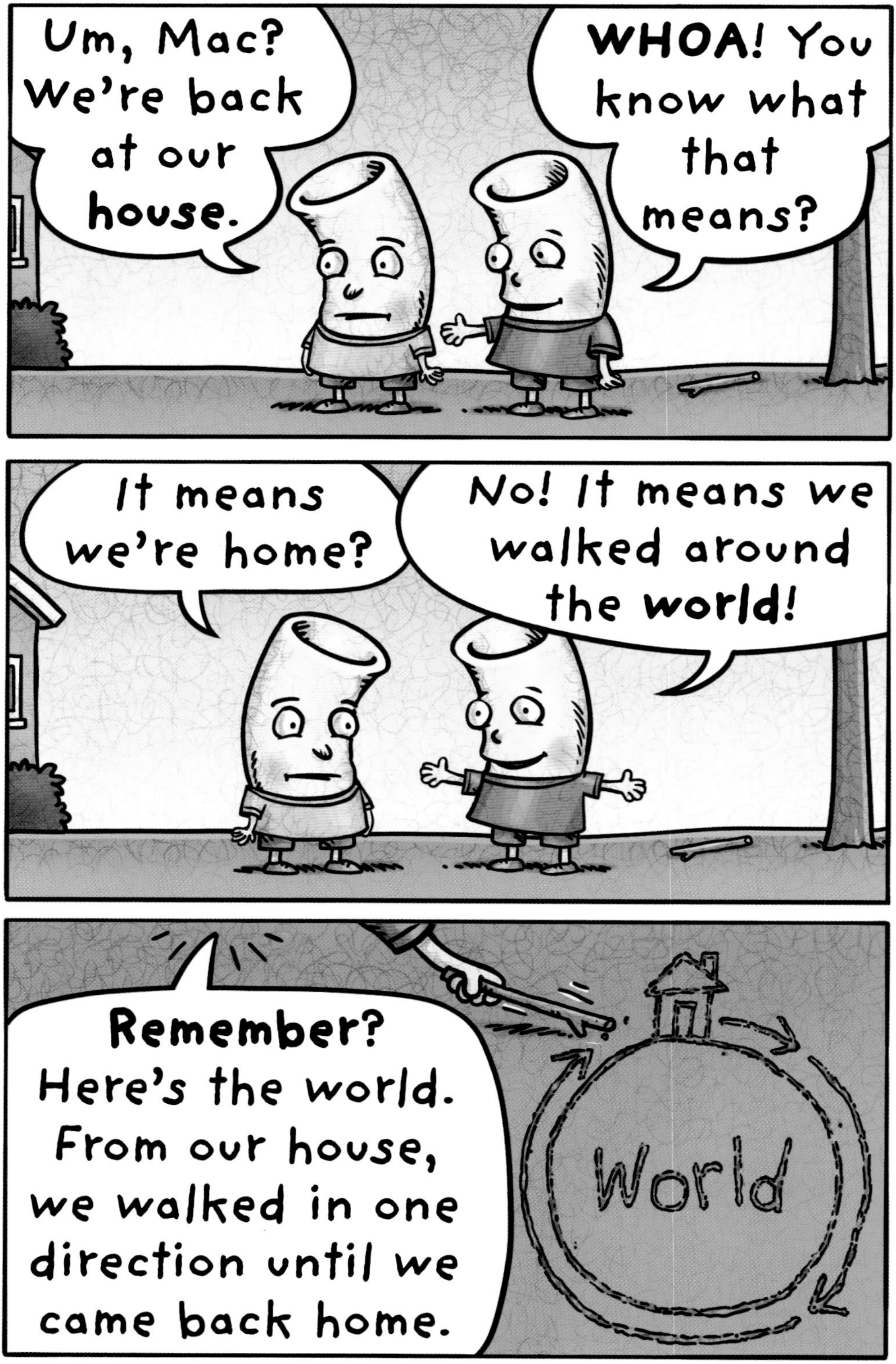
Um, Mac? We're back at our **house.**
WHOA! You know what that means?
It means we're home?
No! It means we walked around the **world!**
Remember?
Here's the world. From our house, we walked in one direction until we came back home.
World

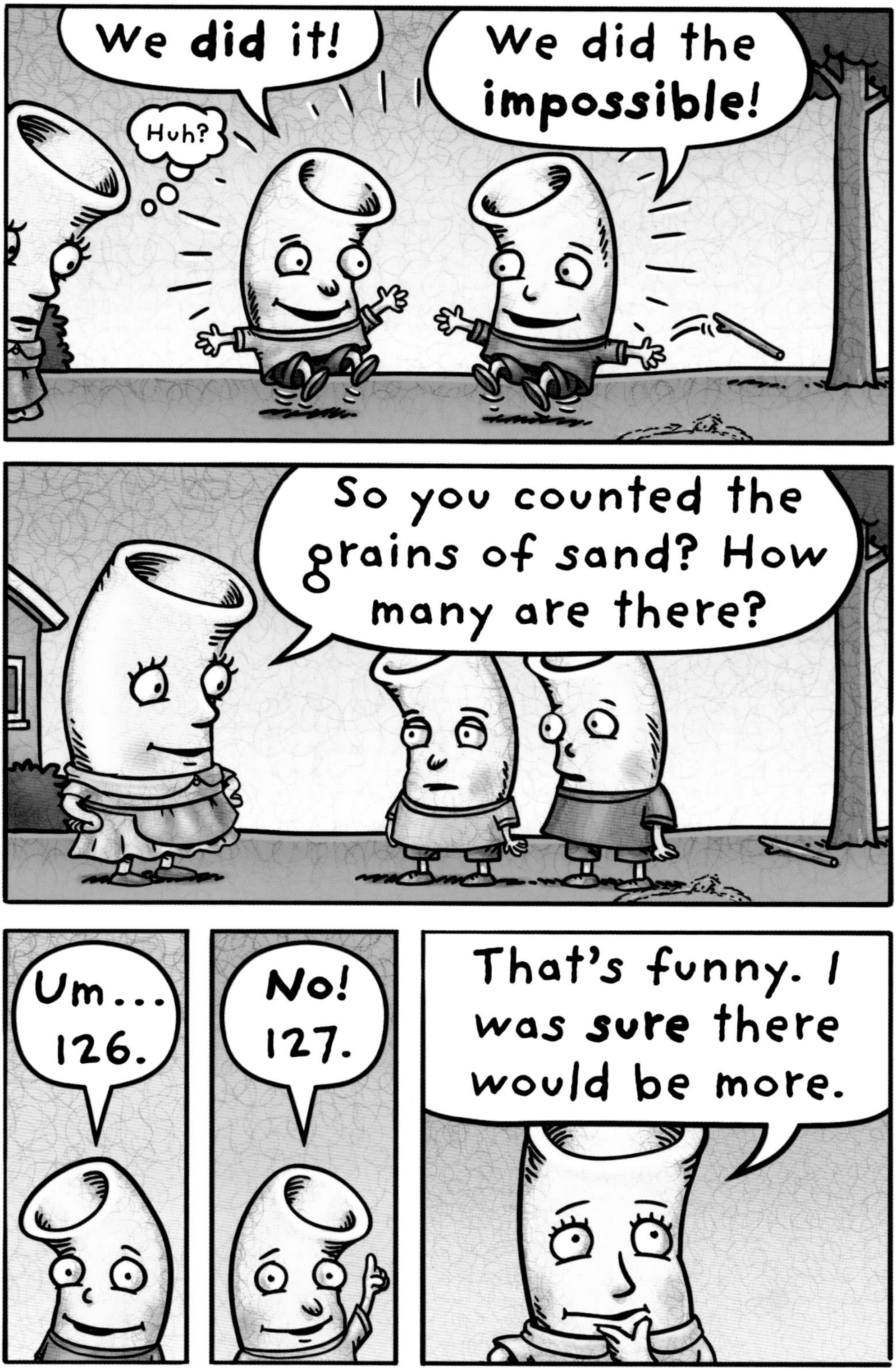

We did it!
We did the impossible!
Huh?
So you counted the grains of sand? How many are there?
Um... 126.
No! 127.
That's funny. I was sure there would be more.

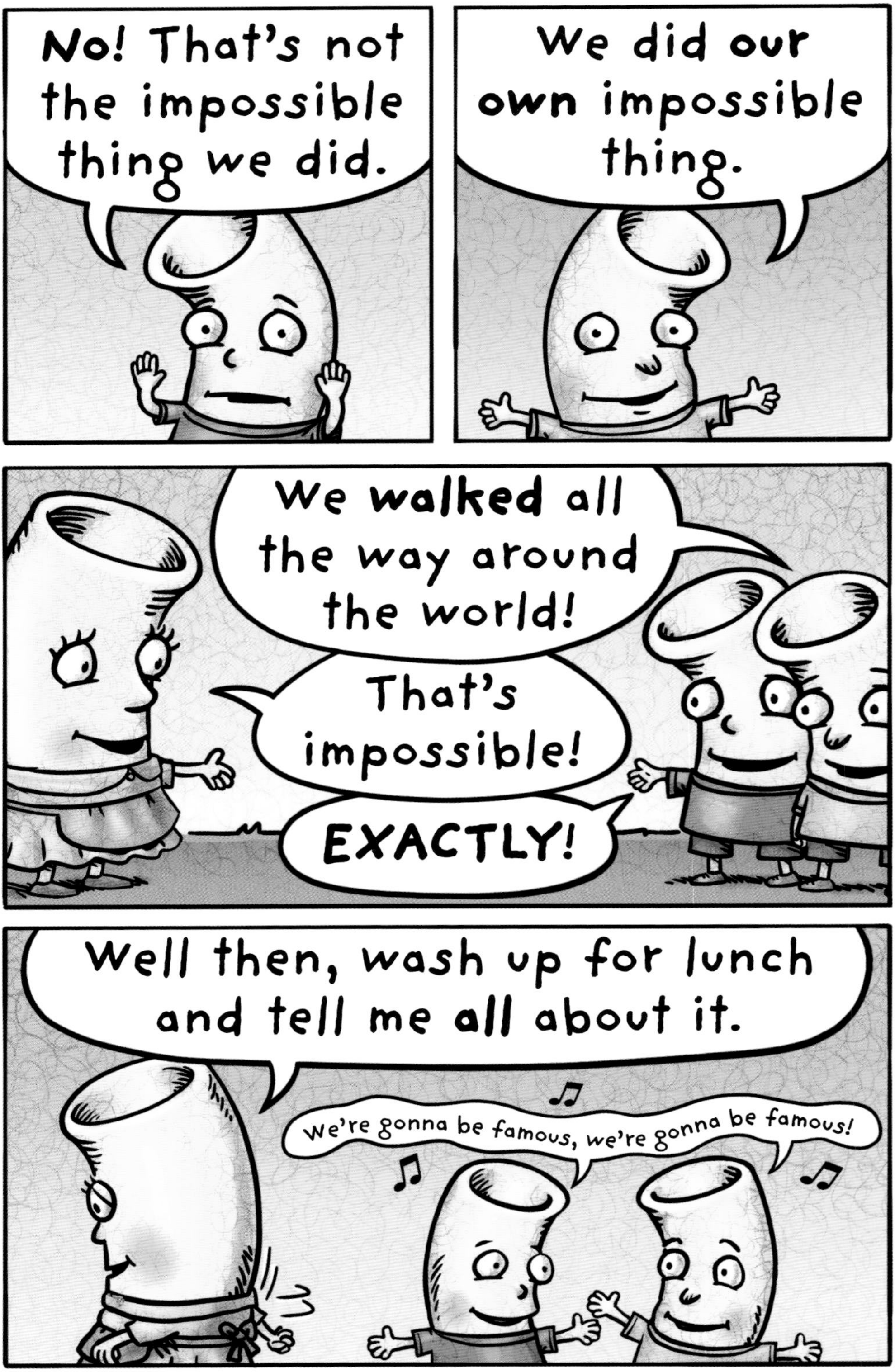
No! That's not the impossible thing we did.
We did our own impossible thing.
We walked all the way around the world!
That's impossible!
EXACTLY!
Well then, wash up for lunch and tell me all about it.
We're gonna be famous, we're gonna be famous!

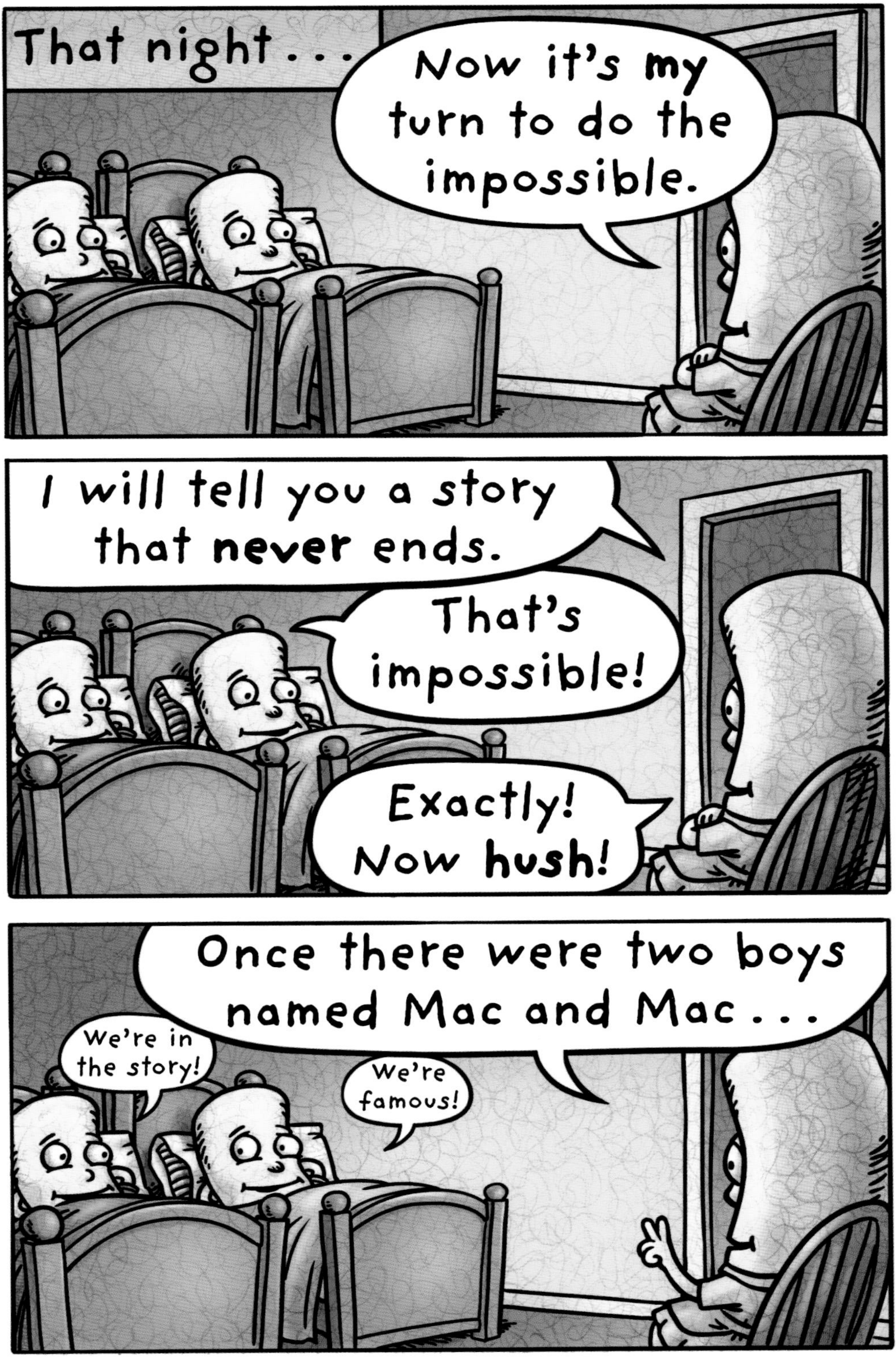

That night . . .
Now it's my turn to do the impossible.
I will tell you a story that never ends.
That's impossible!
Exactly! Now hush!
Once there were two boys named Mac and Mac . . .
We're in the story!
We're famous!

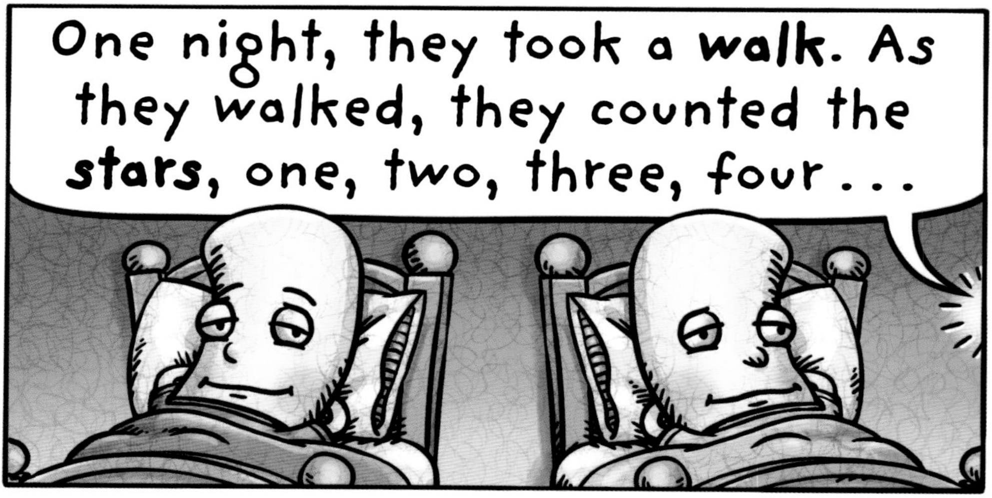
One night, they took a **walk**. As they walked, they counted the **stars**, one, two, three, four . . .

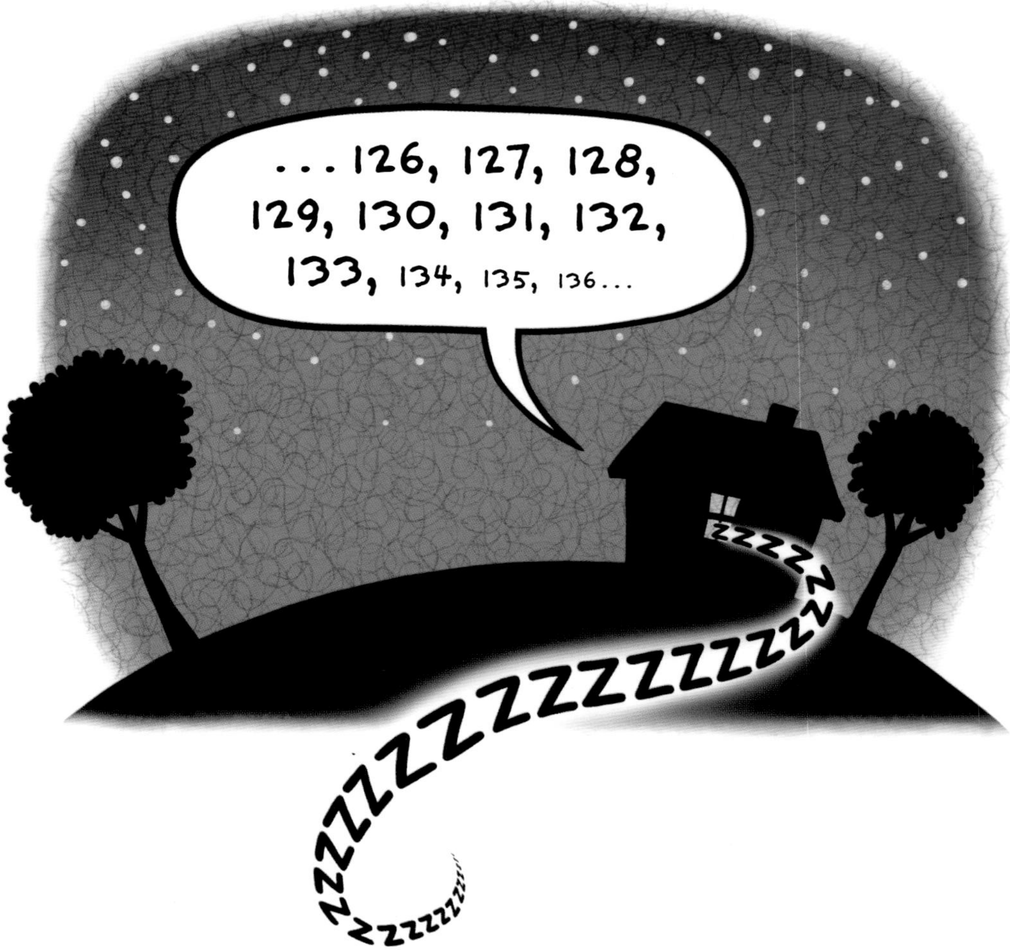
. . . 126, 127, 128, 129, 130, 131, 132, 133, 134, 135, 136 . . .

Authors' Notes

Story Sources for *Noodleheads Do the Impossible*

Old tales about fools, who were also called "noodles" or "noodleheads," are the inspiration for Mac and Mac's adventures in our Noodleheads series. In 1888, W. A. Clouston wrote a scholarly book called *The Book of Noodles* in which he described numerous stories that had been told for hundreds of years and quite a few dating back over two millennia. People around the world tell similar stories about their particular fools, such as Giufà in Italy, Nasr-ed-Din Hodja in Turkey, Juan Bobo in Puerto Rico, and Jack in England. These world tales remind us of our shared humanity; we have all done or said something foolish, and the stories give us a chance to laugh at ourselves. In spite of their foolishness, things usually turn out fine in the end for the fools in these old tales, perhaps because they are generally kind and well-meaning. Children find comfort in the fact that a foolish mistake usually doesn't mean the end of the world. Even if Mac and Mac don't learn from their mistakes, children who read about their adventures do. Noodlehead stories also help them understand humor, logical thinking, and the importance of distinguishing between what's true and what's a lie. Children quickly see that they should not always believe what they hear, especially when the source is a bully like Mac and Mac's "frenemy," Meatball, or Uncle Ziti, who loves to tell tall tales.

World folktales reflect the fact that people have long been fascinated with the idea of doing the impossible. World history is full of true stories of people who did what seemed impossible at the time, such as Magellan circumnavigating Earth or people walking on the moon. And if our Noodleheads, Mac and Mac, decided to do something impossible, we knew that it would also need to be utterly ridiculous, even though they could find a way to make it seem perfectly logical.

The motifs to which we refer in the information that follows are from *The Storyteller's Sourcebook: A Subject, Title, and Motif Index to Folklore Collections for Children* by Margaret Read MacDonald, first edition (Detroit: Gale, 1982), and second edition by Margaret Read MacDonald and Brian W. Sturm (Detroit: Gale, 2001). Tale types are from *A Guide to Folktales in the English Language* by D. L. Ashliman (NY: Greenwood, 1987).

Introduction

The story that inspired this incident is a tall tale told by fishermen throughout North America. Master storyteller Jon Spelman's version can be found in *More Ready-to-Tell Tales From Around the World*, edited by David Holt and Bill Mooney (Little Rock: August House, 2000), pp. 97–99. A recording of him telling it can be found at: https://jonspelman .bandcamp.com/track/the-snake-and-the-frog.

Chapter One: Walk the Walk

The idea of walking around the world seems impossible given the problems caused by, as Mac says, "oceans and cliffs and quicksand and stuff." However, this has not stopped humans from being fascinated with the idea and trying to overcome the obstacles. With encouragement from Thomas Jefferson, John Ledyard set out to walk around the world in

1786: https://unrememberedhistory.com/2016/01/27/the-man-who-tried-to-walk-around-the-world/. Although Ledyard did not complete the trip, others have, as documented by Guinness World Records: https://www.guinnessworldrecords.com/world-records/first-circumnavigation-by-walking/. Paul Salopek is currently walking around the world: https://www.nationalgeographic.org/projects/out-of-eden-walk/#section-0. This chapter offers opportunities to familiarize children with several idioms: "Put your heads together," "Put your best foot forward," and "Don't just talk the talk; you have to walk the walk." Also, when Mac says, "No, but I can hear the ocean," you may need to explain the folk myth that you can hear the ocean when you hold your ear to a conch shell. What you hear is caused by the hollow cavity of the shell amplifying any ambient sounds.

Chapter Two: Seeing Stars

The motifs that inspired these incidents are J1791, *Reflection in water thought to be original of the thing reflected*, and J1791.2, *Man thinks stars reflected in water will drown*. A brief version, "Stars in the Water," can be found in *The Man in the Moon: Sky Tales from Many Lands* by Alta Jablow and Carl Withers (NY: Holt, Rinehart & Winston, 1969), p. 76. More common versions involve rescuing the moon. Mitch and Martha's retelling of a Turkish version, "The Night the Moon Fell into the Well," can be found in *Stories in My Pocket: Tales Kids Can Tell* (Golden, CO: Fulcrum Publishing, 1996), pp. 31–32.

Chapter Three: Follow Your Shoes

The idea for Uncle Ziti to say, "There are as many stars as there are grains of sand," came from numerous world tales where a person who has been given an impossible task counters with another impossibility. The motif is H702, *Riddle: How many stars in the heavens?* The answers range from "as many as the grains of sand" to "as many as the leaves on a tree" or "as many as the hairs on my donkey." A useful picture book for discussing the mind-boggling concept of infinity with children (ages 5–10) is *Infinity and Me* by Kate Hosford, illustrated by Gabi Swiatkowska (Minneapolis: Carolrhoda Books, 2012). The motif for the shoe incident is J2014.2, *Fool sets shoes pointing toward destination*. Our favorite version is "When Shlemiel Went to Warsaw" by Isaac Bashevis Singer from *When Shlemiel Went to Warsaw and Other Stories* (NY: Dell Yearling, 1968), pp. 99–116. Endless tales (Motif Z11, tale type 2300) follow a formula in which a sequence of the same words and/or the same incident are repeated until the audience can no longer bear the repetition. Mac and Mac's mom combines an endless tale with the idea of tricking someone by putting Mac and Mac to sleep with a boring story (Motif A758, *Raven puts bear to sleep with stories*). A version from the Kutchin people, "Fox and Raven Steal the Moon," can be found in *The Man in the Moon: Sky Tales from Many Lands* by Alta Jablow and Carl Withers (NY: Holt, Rinehart & Winston, 1969), pp. 39–40. After trying on Mac's and Mac's shoes and finding the shoes don't fit, Meatball says, "Oh, well. They're too smelly anyway." Someone might say "sour grapes" to describe Meatball's reaction. To explain this common expression, have children read a version of the Aesop fable "Sour Grapes" (Motif J87, *The fox and the sour grapes*). The fox, after failing to reach a bunch of grapes on an arbor, finally gives up and says, "They were probably sour anyway." This is exactly what Meatball does with the shoes.

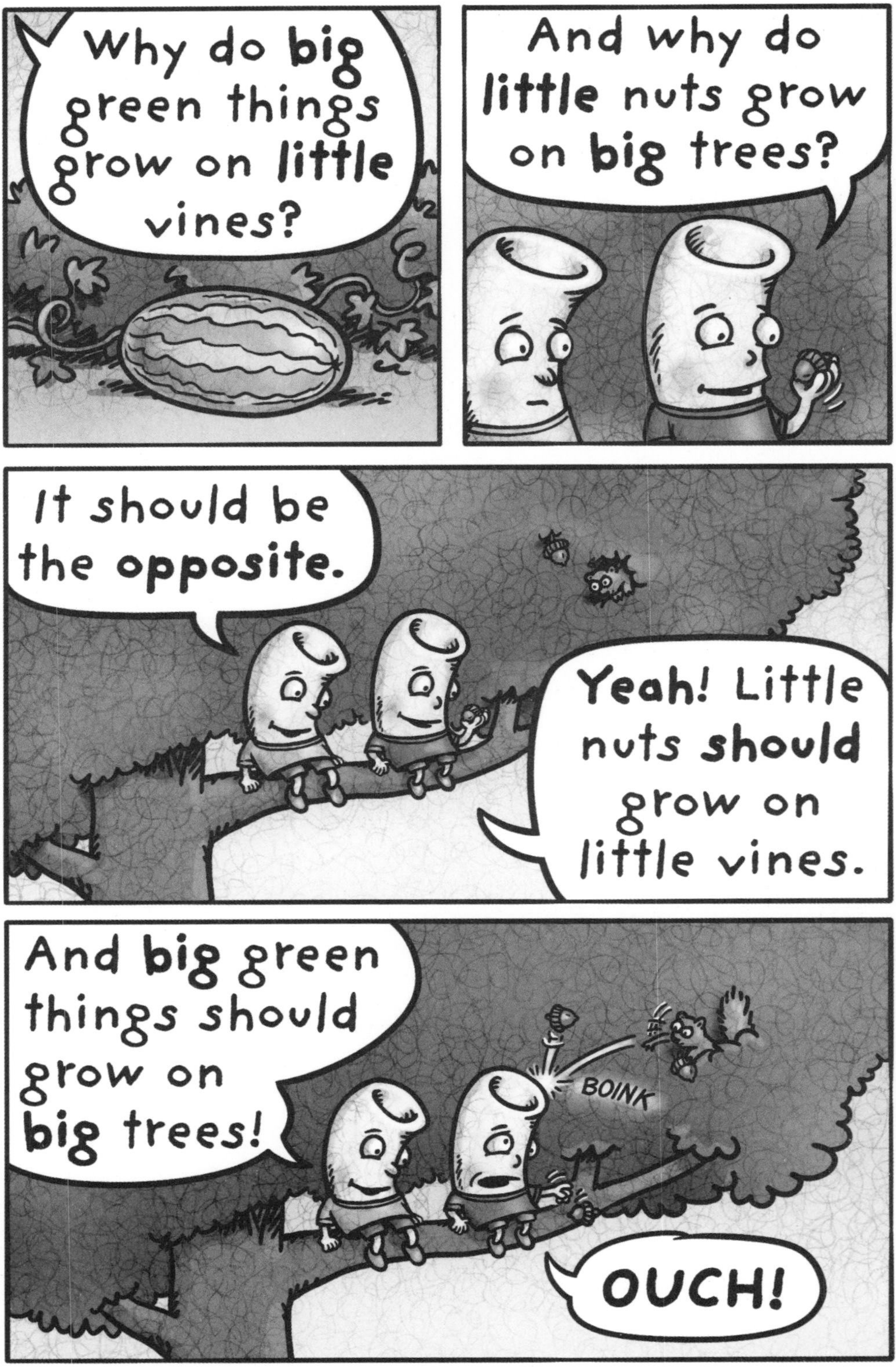
Why do big green things grow on little vines?
And why do little nuts grow on big trees?
It should be the opposite.
Yeah! Little nuts should grow on little vines.
And big green things should grow on big trees!
BOINK
OUCH!